Tales Of The Clipper Ships

by

C. Fox Smith

Tales Of The Clipper Ships
by C. Fox Smith

ISBN: 978-93-68096-91-7

Published by

DOUBLE 9 BOOKS

2/13-B, Ansari Road
Daryaganj, New Delhi – 110002
info@double9books.com
www.double9books.com
Tel. 011-40042856

This book is under public domain

ABOUT THE AUTHOR

C. Fox Smith was a British author and poet known for her vivid storytelling and passion for maritime themes. She developed a deep interest in the sea and sailing, which greatly influenced her writing. Smith is particularly celebrated for her historical fiction and narratives that capture the spirit of the clipper ship era, a time characterized by the grace and speed of sailing vessels.

Her work often reflects her extensive knowledge of nautical history, infused with rich detail and an appreciation for the lives of sailors and their adventures. Smith's writing is marked by its lyrical quality, bringing to life the romance and challenges of life at sea.

In addition to Tales of the Clipper Ships, she published numerous short stories and poems throughout her career. Despite her significant contributions to maritime literature, she remains less known in contemporary literary discussions, yet her work continues to resonate with fans of nautical tales and history.

CONTENTS

THE LAST VOYAGE OF THE "MAID OF ATHENS"

I

OLD Thomas Featherstone was dead: he was also buried.

The knot of frowsy females—that strange and ghoulish sisterhood which frequents such dismal spots as faithfully as dramatic critics the first nights of theatres—who stood monotonously rocking perambulators on their back wheels outside the cemetery gates, were unanimously of opinion that it had been a skinny show. Indeed, Mrs. Wilkins, who was by way of considering herself what reporters like to call the "doyenne" of the gathering, said as much by way of consolation to her special crony Mrs. Pettefer, coming up hot and breathless, five minutes too late for the afternoon's entertainment.

"No flars" (thus Mrs. Wilkins), "not one! Not so much as a w'ite chrysant'! You 'aven't missed much, me dear, I tell you."

Mrs. Pettefer, her hand to her heaving bosom, said there was some called it waste, to be sure, but she did like to see flars 'erself.

"You'd otter'ave seen 'em when they buried the lickle girl yesterday," pursued Mrs. Wilkins.

"I *was* put out, missin' that, but there, I 'ad to take ar Florence to the 'orspittle for 'er aneroids," sighed Mrs. Pettefer, glancing malevolently at "ar Florence" as if she would gladly have buried her, without flars, too, by way of paying her out. "I do love a lickle child's fruneral."

"Mask o' flars, the corfin was," went on Mrs. Wilkins. "The harum lilies was lovely. And one big reaf like an 'arp. W'ite ribbinks on the 'orses, an' all...."

The connoisseurs in grief dispersed. The driver of the hearse replaced the black gloves of ceremony by the woollen ones of comfort, for the day was raw and promised fog later: pulled out a short clay and lit it, climbed to his box and, whipping up his horses (bays with black points—"none of your damned prancing Belgians for me," had been one of Old Featherstone's last injunctions), set off at a brisk trot, he to tea and onions over the stables, they to the pleasant warmth of their stalls and their waiting oats and hay. Four of old Thomas's nearest relatives piled into the first carriage, four more of his remoter kindred into the second, and the lawyer—Hobbs, Senior, of Hobbs, Keating & Hobbs, of Chancery Lane—who had lingered behind to settle accounts with the officiating clergyman, came hurrying down the path between ranks of tombstones, glimmering pale and ghostly in the greying November afternoon, to make up a mixed bag in the third and last with Captain David Broughton, master of the deceased's ship "Maid of Athens," and Mr. Jenkinson, the managing clerk from the office in Billiter Square.

The lawyer was a small, spare man, halting a little from sciatica. Given a pepper-and-salt coat with wide tails, and a straw in his mouth, he would have filled the part of a racing tipster to perfection; but in his sombre funeral array, with his knowing, birdlike way of holding his head, and his sharp, darting, observant glance, he resembled nothing so much as a lame starling; and he chattered like a starling, too, as the carriage rattled away in the wake of the others through the darkening streets towards the respectable northern suburb where old Featherstone had lived and died.

"Sorry to keep you waiting, gentlemen," he said, settling himself in his place as the coachman slammed the door on the party. "Well, well ... everything's passed off very nicely, don't you think?"

Both Captain Broughton and Mr. Jenkinson, after due consideration, agreed that "it" had passed off very nicely indeed; though, to be sure, it would be hard to say precisely what conceivable circumstance might have occurred to make it do otherwise.

Little Jenkinson sat with his back to the horses. He was the kind of person who sits with his back to the horses all through life: the kind of neat, punctual little man to be found in its thousands in the business offices of the City. He carried, as it were, a perpetual pen behind his ear. A clerk to his finger-tips—say that of him, and you have said all; unless perhaps that in private life he was very likely a bit of a domestic tyrant in some brick box of a semi-detached villa Tooting or Balham way, who ran his finger along the sideboard every morning to see if his wife had dusted it properly.

Captain Broughton sat stiffly erect in the opposite corner of the carriage, with its musty aroma of essence-of-funerals—that indescribable blend of new black clothes and moth-balls and damp horsehair and smelling salts and faded flowers. His square hands, cramped into unaccustomed black kid gloves which already showed a white split across the knuckles, lay awkwardly, palms uppermost, on his knees. "Damn the things," he said to himself for the fiftieth time, contemplating their empty finger-tips, sticking out flat as the ends of half-filled pea-pods, "why don't they make 'em so that a man can get his hands into 'em?"

A square-set man, a shade under medium height, with a neat beard, once fair, now faded to a sandy grey, and eyes of the clear ice-blue which suggested a Scandinavian ancestry, he carried his sixty-odd years well. A typical shipmaster, one would say at a first glance: a steady man, a safe man, from whom nothing unexpected need be looked for, one way or the other. And then, perhaps, those ice-blue eyes would give you pause, and the thought would cross your mind that there might be certain circumstances in which the owner of those eyes might conceivably become no longer a safe and steady quantity, but an unknown and even an uncomfortable one.

"Don't mind admitting I'm glad it's over," rattled on the little lawyer; "depressing affairs, these funerals, to my thinking. Horrible. Good for business, though—our business and doctors' business, what! More people get their death through attendin' other people's funerals than one likes to think of. It's the standing, you know. That's what does it. Standing on damp ground. Nothing worse—nothing! And then no hats. That's where our friends the Jews have the pull of us Gentiles—eh, Mr. Jenkinson? If a Jew wants to show respect, he keeps his hat on. Curious, ain't it? Ever hear the story about the feller—Spurgeon, was it—or Dr. Parker—Spurgeon, I think—one or t'other of 'em, anyway, don't much matter, really—and the two fellers that kept their hats on while he was preachin'? 'If I were to go to a synagogue,' says Spurgeon—yes, I'm pretty sure it was Spurgeon—'if I went to a synagogue,' says he, 'I should keep my hat on; and therefore I should be glad if those two young Jews in the back of the church would take theirs off in *my* synagogue'—ha ha ha—good, wasn't it?...

"And talking about getting cold at funerals, I'll let you into a little secret. I always wear an extra singlet, myself, for funerals. Yes; and a body belt. Got 'em on now. Fact. My wife laughs at me. But I say, 'Oh, you may laugh, my dear, but you'd laugh the other side of your face if I came home with lumbago and you had to sit up half the night ironing my back.' Ever try that for lumbago? A common flat iron—*you* know. Hot as you can bear it. Best thing going—ab-so-lutely...."

He paused while he rubbed a clear place in the windows which their breath had misted and peered out like a child going to a party.

"Nearly there, I think," he went on. "Between ourselves, I think the old gentleman's going to cut up remarkably well. Six figures, I shouldn't wonder. Not a bit, I shouldn't.... A shrewd man, Captain Broughton, don't you agree?"

Captain Broughton in his dark corner made a vague noise which might be taken to indicate that he did agree. Not that it mattered, really, whether he agreed or not. The little lawyer was one of those people who was so fond of hearing his own voice that he never even noticed if anyone was listening to him; which was all to the good when you were feverishly busy with your own thoughts.

"Ah, yes," he resumed, "a very shrewd, capable man of business! Saw the way things were going in the shipping world and got out in time. 'The sailing ship is done' (those were his very words to me). 'If I'd been thirty years younger I'd have started a fleet of steam kettles with the best of 'em. But not now—not at my time of life. You can't teach an old dog new tricks.' Those were his very words....

"Ah, ha, here we are at last! Between ourselves, a glass o' the old gentleman's port won't come amiss. Fine cellar he kept—fine cellar! 'I don't go in for a lot of show, Hobbs,' I remember him saying once, 'but I like what I have *good*....'"

II

Old Featherstone's home was a dull, ugly, solid, inconvenient Victorian house in a dull crescent of similar houses. It stands there still—it has been more fortunate than Featherstone's Wharf in Limehouse and the little dark office in Billiter Square with "T. Featherstone" on its dusty wire blinds and the half model of the "Parisina" facing you as you went in. They are gone; but the house I saw only the other day—its rhododendrons perhaps a shade dingier, a trifle more straggly, and "bright young society" (for the place is a select boarding establishment for City gents nowadays) gyrating to the blare of a loudspeaker in what was aforetime old Thomas Featherstone's dining-room. And the legend "Pulo Way," in tarnished gilt on black, still gleams in the light of the street lamp opposite on the two square stone gateposts— bringing a sudden momentary vision of dark seas and strange stars, of ships becalmed under the lee of the land, of light puffs of warm, spicy air stealing out from unseen shores as if they breathed fragrance in their sleep; so that the vague shapes of "Lyndhurst" and "Chatsworth" and "Bellavista" seem the humped outlines of islands sheltering one knows not what of wonder and peril and romance....

A maidservant had come in and lighted the gas in the dining-room, lowered the drab venetian blinds in the bay window, and drawn the heavy stamped plush curtains which hung stiffly under the gilt cornice. Broughton sipped his glass of wine and ate a sandwich, surveying the familiar room with that curious illogical sense of surprised resentment which humanity always feels in the presence of the calm indifference of inanimate things to its own transiency and mortality.

He knew it well, that rather gloomy apartment with its solid Victorian air of ugly, substantial comfort. He had been there before many times. It had been one of Thomas Featherstone's unvarying customs to invite his skippers to a ceremonial dinner whenever their ships were in London River. An awful sort of business, Broughton had always secretly thought these functions; and, like the lawyer on the present occasion, had been heartily glad when they were over. The bill of fare never varied—roast beef, baked potatoes, some kind of a boiled pudding, almonds and raisins, and a bottle of port to follow. "Special Captain's port," that turbulent Irishman, Pat Shaughnessy, of the "Mazeppa," irreverently termed it: adding, with his great laugh, "You bet the old divvle don't fetch out his best vintage for hairy shellbacks like us!"

Thirteen—no, it must be fourteen—of those dinners Broughton could remember. They had been annual affairs so long as the "Maid of Athens" could hold her own against the steamers in the Australian wool trade. Latterly, since she had been driven to tramping the world for charters, they had become movable feasts, and between the last two there had been a gap of nearly three years.

Broughton's eyes travelled slowly from one detail to another—the mahogany chairs ranged at precise intervals against the dull red of the flock-papered walls; the round table whose gleaming brass toes peeped modestly from beneath the voluminous tapestry table cover; the "lady's and gent's easies" sitting primly on opposite sides of the vast yawning cavern of the fire-place; the mantelpiece where the black marble clock ticked leisurely between its flanking Marly horses and the pair of pagoda vases, with their smirking ladies and fierce bewhiskered warriors, that one of the old man's captains had brought years ago from Foochow; the mahogany sideboard whose plate-glass mirror gave back every minutest detail of the room in reverse; the inlaid glass-fronted bookcase with its smug rows of gilt-tooled, leather-bound books—the Waverley Novels, Falconer's "Shipwreck," Byron's poems.

Thomas Featherstone seldom used any other room but this. He possessed a drawing-room: a bleak chill shrine of the middle-class elegancies where the twittering Victorian niece who kept house for him—a characterless worthy woman with the red nose which bespeaks a defective digestion—was wont to dispense tepid tea and flabby muffins on her periodical "At Home" days. He had no study: he had his office for his work, he said, and that was enough for him. He had been brought up to sit in the dining-room at home in his father's, the ship-chandler's, house in Stepney, and he had carried the custom with him into the days of his prosperity.

So there he had sat, evening after evening, with his gold spectacles perched on his high nose, reading "Lloyd's List" and the commercial columns of "The Times," the current issues of which were even now in the brass newspaper rack by his empty chair: occasionally playing a hand of picquet with the twittering niece. He was a man of an almost inhuman punctuality of habit. People had been known to set their watches by Old Featherstone. At nine o'clock every morning of the week round came the brougham to drive him into the City. At twelve o'clock he sallied forth from Billiter Square to the "London Tavern," and the table that he always occupied there. At half-past one, back to the office; or, if one of his ships were due, to the West India Docks, where they generally berthed. At five the brougham appeared in Billiter Square to transport him to "Pulo Way" again.

A strange, colourless, monotonous sort of life, one would think; and one which had singularly little in common with the wider aspects of the business in which his money had been made. Of the romantic side of shipping, or indeed of its human side, he seemed to have no conception at all. A consignment of balas rubies, of white elephants, of Manchester goods, of pig iron, they were all one to him—so many items in a bill of lading, no more, no less. Ships carried his house-flag to the four corners of the earth: no one of them had ever carried him farther than the outward-bound pilot. No matter what outlandish ports they visited, it stirred his blood not a whit. Perhaps it was one of the secrets of his success: for imagination, nine times out of ten, is a dangerous sort of commodity, commercially considered; and if Old Featherstone had gone a-gallivanting off to Tuticorin or Amoy or Punta Arenas or Penang or Port au Prince or any other alluringly-named place with which his ships trafficked, instead of sitting in Billiter Square and looking after his business—why, no doubt his business would have been vastly the sufferer! And, indeed, since he found such adventure as his soul needed no farther afield than between the marbled covers of his own ledgers, there would have been no sense in looking for it elsewhere.

You saw the old man's portrait yonder over the mantelpiece, behind the marble clock and the Marly horses—keen eyes under bushy eyebrows, side whiskers, Gladstone collar, slightly sardonic smile. Broughton indulged in a passing speculation as to what they did with his glass eye when they buried him. The picture was the work of an unknown artist. "If I'd been fool enough to pay for a big name," old Thomas had been wont to say, "I'd have got a worse picture for three times the money"; and the old man had not forgotten to drive a hard bargain, the recollection of which had perhaps a little coloured the artist's mood. The unknown had caught his sitter in a characteristic attitude: sitting erect and rigid, his hands clasped one above the other on the silver knob of his favourite Malacca walking-stick. A shrewd old man, you would say, a shrewd, hard, narrow old man, and not have been far wrong in your estimate; though, as even his enemies were bound to admit, he was not without his moments of vision, his odd surprising streaks of generosity.

A man of but little education—he had run as a child daily to a little school in Stepney, kept by the widow and daughters of a shipmaster, and later had gone for a year or two to an Academy for the Sons of Gentlemen somewhere off the East India Dock Road—he was wont to say, and to say as if it were something to boast of, that he had never read but two books in his life—Falconer's "Shipwreck" and Byron's poems, both of which he knew from cover to cover. For the latter he had a profound and astonishing admiration, so much so that all his ships were named after Byronic heroes and heroines.

The "junk store" some wag once called the Featherstone fleet: and the gibe was not far wide of the mark. Anyone who has the patience and the curiosity to search the pages of a fifty-or sixty-year-old "Lloyd's Register" will find in that melancholy record of human achievement and human effort blown like dead leaves on the winds of time and change sufficient reason for the nickname. Everywhere it is the same tale—"Mazeppa" *ex* "Electric Telegraph," "Bride of Abydos" *ex* "Navarino," "Zuleika" *ex* "Roderick Random," "Thyrza" *ex* "Rebel Maid." Old Featherstone had at one time more than fifty ships under his house-flag, not one of which had been built to his order. "The man who succeeds," was one of his sayings, "is the man who knows best how to profit by other men's mistakes."

The doctrine was one which he put very effectively into practice. He had an almost uncanny nose for bargains; but, what was more than that, he was gifted in a most amazing degree with that peculiar and indefinable quality best described as "ship sense"—an ability amounting well-nigh to a genius for knowing a good ship from a bad one which is seldom found but in seamen, and is rare even among them.

Someone once asked him the secret of his gift, but I doubt if he got much satisfaction out of the answer.

"Ask me another," snapped out the old man in his dry, staccato fashion. "I've got a brother can waggle his ears like a jackass. How does *he* do that? *I* don't know. *He* don't know. Same thing in my case, exactly."

And certainly where he got it is something of a mystery. But since there had been Featherstones buried for generations where time and grime combine to make a hallowed shade in the old parish church of Stepney, there may well have been seafaring blood in the family, and likely enough the founder of the little bow-windowed shop in Wapping Wall was himself a retired ship's carpenter.

Whatever the explanation, there was undeniably the fact. He bought steamers that didn't pay and had never paid and that experts said never would pay: ripped the guts out of them, and in a couple of years they had paid for themselves. He bought unlucky ships, difficult ships, ships with a bad name of every sort and kind. Ships that broke their captains' hearts and their owners' fortunes, ships that wouldn't steer, that wouldn't wear, that wouldn't stay. And never once did his bargain turn out a bad one.

III

From Old Featherstone's portrait, and that painted ironical smile which still had the power to call up in him a feeling of vague discomfort, Broughton's eyes travelled on to the portraits of ships which—Old Featherstone excepted—were the room's sole artistic adornment.

Over there in the corners—one each side of the portrait—were the old "Childe Harold" and "Don Juan." They were the first ships Old Featherstone bought, in the distant days when he was still young Featherstone, a smart young clerk in Daly's office, whose astonishing rise to fortune was yet on the knees of the gods.

They were old frigate-built East Indiamen, both of them, the "General Bunbury" and "Earl Clapham," from some Bombay or Moulmein dockyard: teak through and through, but as leaky as sieves with sheer age and years of labouring in seaways. Young Featherstone bought them for a song: gutted them, packed their roomy 'tween-decks with emigrants like herrings in a barrel, and hurried them backwards and forwards as fast as he dared between London and Australia while the gold rush of the 'sixties was at its hottest. He was in too big a hurry even to give them new figureheads to match their new names, with the result that a portly British general and a highly respectable peer of Evangelistic tendencies had to endure the indignity of an enforced masquerade, the one as the wandering "Childe," the other as the disreputable "Don" of many amours.

Goodness knows how these two old ships' venerable ribs managed to stick together running down the Easting: nor indeed how it was that they didn't carry their freight of hopeful fortune seekers to the bottom before they were well clear of the Channel. However, by hook or by crook, stick together they did, long enough at any rate to lay the foundation of Featherstone's success. The "Childe Harold"—she who was the "General Bunbury"—created a bit of a sensation in the last lap of her third voyage by sinking, poor old soul, in the West India Dock entrance at the head of a whole fleet of shipping crowding in on the tide. The "Don Juan"—the backsliding "Earl Clapham"—came to grief, by a stroke of luck, just off the Mauritius, and her old bones (it must have taken a small forest of teak to build her) fetched double what Featherstone had paid for her for building material. But they had served their purpose. Thereafter, Featherstone never looked behind him.

The old "Giaour"—*she* started life as a steamer, in the days when steam was suffering from over-inflation, and a good many speculators were scalding their fingers badly with it. The "Cottonopolis," of the defunct "Spreadeagle" Line—that was how she began. Her accommodation was the talk of the town, said to be the most lavish ever seen—a wash basin to every six cabins—but she devoured such quantities of fuel, as well as turning out such a brute in a seaway that her passenger list was never more than half full, that the shareholders were glad to get rid of her at a loss. There she was—an ugly great lump of a ship, with masts that had a peculiar rake to them, something after the style of a Chinese junk. Sail, too ... like a witch, she did!... Then the little "Thyrza"—*she* was a pretty little butterfly of a thing; but she was as near being a mistake as any purchase Featherstone ever made. He had bought her, so it was believed, with the intention at the back of his mind of winning the China tea race; but the tea trade petering out, he put her into the wool fleet instead. Broughton had seen the dainty little ship many a time: a regular picture she used to look, beating up to the Heads just as old Captain Winter had painted her. Rare hand with a paint-brush that old chap was, and no mistake! Give him one good look at a ship, and he'd get her likeness to a gantline ... notice things about her, too, sometimes, that even her own skipper hadn't found out....

There was the "Manfred"—the unluckiest ship, surely, that ever left the ways! The "Young Tamlin" was the name she used to go by, in the days when she used to kill two or three men every trip. That was before Old Featherstone got hold of her, of course: and her owners—she belonged to a little one-ship company—got the jumps about it and sold her. Sold her cheap, too ... but, bless you, that stopped her gallop all right! She drowned no more men afterwards.

And—last of all—the "Maid of Athens." ...

Broughton's own ship—the pride of his heart, the apple of his eye, the guiding motive, the absorbing interest of his life for more than twenty-five years.

Broughton didn't care much about that picture—never had done, though he didn't trouble to tell the old man so. No use asking for trouble: and he was a contrary old devil if you crossed him! A Chinese ship-chandler's affair, it was, and moreover it showed the "Maid" with a spencer at the main which she never carried: at least, not in Broughton's time. A good long time that meant, too ... ah well! They had grown old together, his ship and he!

He remembered the day he got command of her as clearly as if it were yesterday. He was chief officer of the "Haidée" at the time—getting along in years, too, and beginning to wonder if he would ever have the luck to get a ship of his own. She was a nice little ship, the "Haidée," the last of Daly's fleet, and Featherstone bought her after old Daly, who had given him a stool in his office years before, shot himself in that very office in Fenchurch Street when the news came of the wreck of the "Allan-a-Dale," his favourite ship, on the Calf of Man. Quite a nice little ship, but nothing out of the common about her: nothing a man could take to particularly, somehow. And yet at the time he had wanted nothing better than to be her skipper.

Old Captain Philpot had been queerish all that voyage; he used to nip brandy on the quiet a lot, and take drugs when he could get them as well. Soon after they left the Coromandel coast he went out of his mind altogether, and Broughton found him one day, when he went down to dinner, crawling round the cabin on all fours and complaining that he was King Nebuchadnezzar and couldn't find any grass to eat.

Good Lord! that was a time, too ... made a man sweat to think of it, even after all these years! Hurricane after hurricane right through the Indian Ocean: on deck most of the time, and sitting on the Old Man's head when he got rumbustious during the watch below. However, the poor old chap died as quiet as a child, when he smelt the Western Islands, and Broughton as chief officer took the vessel into port.

Old Featherstone came on board, as his custom was, as soon as she was fairly berthed, and Broughton—tongue-tied and stammering as he always was on important occasions of the kind—gave an account of his stewardship. The old man listened with never a word, only just a grunt or a brusque nod now and again; and when the tale was told made no comment whatever beyond a curt "Humph! Well, you can't have command of this ship. She's promised to Allinson. Can't go back on him. Besides, he's senior to you."

Then, with one foot on the gangway, he turned back and barked out:

"I've bought a new ship. 'Philopena' or some such outlandish name. She's at Griffin's Wharf, Millwall. Better go and look at her. You can have her if you fancy her."

Half-way down the gangway he turned again.

"Come and dine with me at Blackheath on Thursday. Seven o'clock. And don't keep me waiting, mind! I'm a punctual man, or I shouldn't be where I am."

That invitation—invitation? it was more like a Royal command—as Broughton well knew, set the seal on his promotion.

The ship was the "Maid of Athens."

IV

Broughton went in search of her as soon as he had finished up on board the "Haidée" and turned her over to the care of the old lame shipkeeper.

He didn't feel particularly excited; his feeling, naturally enough, was one of pleasurable anticipation of an improvement in his material circumstances—no more than that, as he realized with that wistful sense of flatness and disappointment which inevitably accompanies the discovery that some long-desired consummation has lost through the lapse of time its power to excite and to intoxicate the mind. "If this had happened ten years ago," he thought rather sadly, "Lord, how full of myself I should have been!" forgetting that middle age, when it does make acquaintance with passion, seldom does it by halves.

He found the "Philopena" in a derelict, melancholy wet dock somewhere among vacant lots and chemical works down in the Isle of Dogs, along with a couple of dilapidated coasting colliers and a broken-down tug—a smoky Thames-side sunset burning like a banked fire behind the cynical-looking sheds of a shadowy and problematical Griffin—and he fell in love with her on the instant.

There is—or perhaps one should rather say was, since it is doubtful if the Age of Steam has cognizance of such sentimental weaknesses—a certain kind of thrill, not to be satisfactorily defined in words, which runs through a man's whole being when first his eyes fall upon the one ship which, out of all the thousands which sail the seas, seems especially made to be the complement of his own being, as surely as a woman is made for her mate. It is a feeling to which first love is perhaps the thing most nearly comparable—it can make the most commonplace of men into a poet; and even that lacks one of its qualities—its pure and sexless virginity. Other ships there may be more beautiful; but they leave him cold. They are not for him as she is for him....

That thrill it was—that awakening of two of the root instincts of mankind, the instinct to cherish, and the instinct to possess—which ran (surprising even himself) through that most matter-of-fact and unimaginative of men, David Broughton, when he first set eyes on the ship that for twenty-odd years to come was destined to provide the main interest and object of his existence.

There seemed to be nobody about the wharf, but Broughton untied a leaky dinghy that he found moored under the piles and pulled out to her. The nearer he got to her the better he liked her. Stern a bit on the heavy side, he fancied—with too much weight aft she'd be inclined to run up into the wind if you didn't watch her. She'd want some handling, all right, but it wouldn't do to be afraid of her, either. Her lines were a dream! He pulled all round her, viewing her from every angle; and as he rowed under her keen bow he caught himself fancying that her little dainty figurehead looked down upon him with a kind of wistful appeal—a sort of "You won't go away and leave me, will you?" look that won his heart on the spot.

He made the boat fast to the crazy Jacob's ladder and swung himself on board. She was filthily dirty, appallingly neglected, with that unspeakably forlorn and abandoned look which ships seem to get after a long lay-up in port. The grime and litter everywhere made his heart ache. The Dagoes had had her for the last year or two, and her little cabin reeked of garlic and stale cigar smoke. The shipkeeper, a drink-sodden old ruffian with a horrible red-running eye, who was probably none too pleased at the prospect of losing his job now his temporary home was sold, followed Broughton round grumbling and croaking. Lor' bless you, *she* wouldn't sail, not she! No more'n a mule'll go if he don't want to! There was plenty had had a try at her, and they all told the same tale. Somethink wrong with the way she was built, must be ... or else they'd laid her keel of a Friday or summat....

Broughton smiled to himself. Somehow, he thought, that ship was going to sail for him! He couldn't have explained the feeling for the life of him, but there it was.

And so, in point of fact, things turned out. Just as a horse which is an unmanageable fiend in the hands of a crack jockey will let some snip of a stable lad do what he will with him—just as a dog made savage by ill-usage will attach himself for life (and perhaps—who knows?—beyond) to someone who first masters him and then shows him kindness—so did this little wild "Philopena" under her new name of "Maid of Athens" show no sign of the tricks and vices, whatever they might be, which had brought her, like some lovely but wilful lady fallen among evil companions, to the obscene desolation of that forlorn Millwall wet dock. Twenty-five years ago ... ah, well, they had been happy years, on the whole! A reserved and rather lonely man, not over fond of company, Broughton had drifted into a negatively disastrous sort of marriage in his young days with a woman considerably older than himself. With the best will in the world to do so, he had been unable to feel any but a superficial grief at her death a few years later; and in the house where his married stepdaughter now lived he always felt like a stranger on sufferance during his brief periods ashore. But he had found an abiding content in the daily routine of his life at sea. He gave himself up to his ship without grudging. She was his one interest in life, his hobby, his love. He laid out his spare cash on little items of personal adornment for her as for a loved woman, and on the new gear of which Old Featherstone stinted her as his natural tendency to stinginess increased with age.

It was a brother skipper, Tom Pellatt, of Maclean's pretty little clipper "Phoebe Maclean"—a silly, noisy chap Broughton privately thought him—who had first put the idea into his head that the "Maid of Athens" might one day become his own property in name as she already was in spirit.

Pellatt had been dining on board when both ships were in Sydney Harbour, and just as he was going he said:

"Tell you what, Broughton, you've been the making of this ship; and if old Nethermillstone don't leave her to you in his will he damn well ought to, that's all!"

Broughton put the suggestion aside with a laugh. Pellatt, who was one of those people who, as the phrase goes, "talk as they warm," and simply said it out of a desire to say something complimentary and pleasing to his host—Broughton's absorption in his ship being something of a standing joke among his fellow-captains when his back was turned—probably forgot he had ever said it before he got back to his own ship. But the words had sown their seed.

At first Broughton only played with the idea at odd moments: he would do this, he would do that, if the ship were his—treating it as a pleasant kind of game of make-believe wherewith to beguile an idle minute; but always with the mental proviso that, of course, no one but a silly gabbling ass like Pellatt would ever have thought of such a thing.

Then, gradually, he began to wonder if it really was such a ridiculous notion, after all. Old Featherstone's business would die with him, that was very certain. Hadn't he said as much himself, the last time Broughton dined at Blackheath, about the time young Daly, whose father Featherstone had worked for in his clerking days, came such a holy mucker in the Bankruptcy Court?

"I don't intend to leave my house-flag to be trailed through the mire!" he had said.

And hadn't he said, too, not once but many times:

"I shall never sell the 'Maid of Athens'!"

Presently, from being a desirable but remote possibility, he began to consider it in the light of a probability; and from that it was but a short step to take to begin to look upon it as a right. Who, he asked himself, had a stronger claim to the ship than he—if, indeed, half so strong?

He began by degrees to make his plans more definitely. It was no longer "if the ship were mine," but "when she is mine." He hugged the thought to him, fed upon it, lived with it night and day. He hoped he could honestly say he had never wished Old Featherstone's death; but when the news of his death had come he had not been able to repress a thrill of exultation as the thought rose to the surface of his mind, "Now, at last, she will surely be mine!"

It had been the old man himself who had finally turned what had until then been no more than a vague hope into a virtual certainty.

It was on the occasion of that last dinner at Blackheath, a matter of six weeks ago, just before the attack of bronchitis that had finished the old fellow off. There he had sat in his big easy-chair by the fire, looking incredibly frail and shrunken, his eyes, for all that, as keen as ever in their sunken caves as they wandered from Broughton's face to the counterfeit presentment of the "Maid of Athens" riding proudly on her painted sea.

"Well, Broughton," he had snapped out, suddenly, for a moment almost like his old self again, "you've thought a lot of the old ship, haven't you?"

Broughton, taken by surprise, and feeling, no doubt, just a little guilty about those secret aircastles of his, said, stammering, well, yes, he supposed he had.

And there the matter stopped. Not much, perhaps; but straws show which way the wind blows. Broughton thought he was justified in reading a certain significance into the incident.

And again, on the way up to the funeral that morning, he had looked in at a little club he belonged to, and met half a dozen skippers of his acquaintance: always the same tale—"Hello, Broughton! Off to plant old Feathers, I suppose! Hope he's come down handsome in his will."

"Bless you, I'm not expecting anything!" had been Broughton's answer, as much to the jealous Fates as to them.... Well, it would soon be settled now one way or the other. He didn't really, in his heart of hearts, believe in the possibility of that other way at all; but he included it in his mind as a matter of form—again with that vague half-superstitious notion of propitiating some watchful and sardonic Destiny.

He was surprised to find himself so little excited now that the great moment had arrived. He had had to keep a tight hand on himself on the way up from the cemetery, lest he should betray his fever of nervous impatience to his companions, and he had been relieved when the lawyer's constant flow of chatter obviated the necessity of his taking any share in the conversation. Now, he was glad to find, he had got himself well under control. He was even able to derive a certain quiet interest from observing the suppressed eagerness on the decorous countenances of Old Featherstone's relations. A so-so lot, on the whole! Broughton thought by the looks of 'em that old Thomas must have had the lion's share of the family wits.

Funny that a man should spend all his life piling money up, and then have no one to leave it to that he really cared for! "My brother's children'll get my money when I'm gone," Old Featherstone used to say; "don't think much of 'em, but there it is! I hope they'll enjoy spending it as much as I've enjoyed making it." ...

The little lawyer sipped the last of his port, drew his chair up to the table, and rummaged in the depths of his shabby brown bag with the air of grave importance of a conjurer about to produce rabbits from a hat.

Ah, here was the rabbit—a blue, folded paper which he unfolded, flattened with immense deliberation, and began to read in the dead silence which had suddenly fallen on the room.

By George, thought Broughton, the old fellow was warm and no mistake! Houses here, houses there, shares in this railway, that bank, the other mine. It didn't interest him much personally, but it was as good as a play to see the pale gooseberry eyes of that grocer-looking chap bulging with excitement until they bade fair to drop out of his head.

"The house 'Pulo Way' and the contents thereof (with the exception of certain items specified elsewhere)," droned on the lawyer's unmusical, monotonous voice, "to Rosina Barratt for her life." ... Rosina Barratt—that was the dyspeptic niece. Broughton felt glad to know he'd done the proper thing by her. She deserved it. A decent woman: and he must have been a crotchety old devil to live with in his latter days!

Good Lord, what an interminable rigmarole this legal business was! Broughton moved restlessly in his seat. The ships—the ships! Was he never coming to them?

His own name, starting at him out of the midst of the formal phraseology, made his heart miss a beat. Here it was at last: but no—not yet——

"To Captain David Broughton my oil painting of the clipper ship 'Maid of Athens' in gold frame, knowing his regard for the ship and that he will value the painting on that account...."

Broughton just managed to bite back a laugh in time. If the old chap had known what he really thought about that picture!

The lawyer droned on. Somebody got that black clock on the mantelpiece—somebody else the old man's Malacca cane—two hundred pounds to little Jenkinson—a hundred to the lawyer. The little clerk sat up and smirked like a Sunday School kid that hears its name read out for a prize; but the lawyer, Broughton thought not without a touch of amusement, didn't look any too well pleased with his.

The ships—the ships—what about the ships?...

"I desire that my two ships, 'Maid of Athens' and 'Thyrza,' shall be sold within twelve months after my decease, and the proceeds of the sale divided amongst the legatees aforesaid in the same proportion as the rest of my estate."

It seemed to Broughton that the lawyer's respectfully modulated tones went roaring and echoing round the room, with a note of derision in them like the ironical laughter of fiends. A black mist swam before his eyes for a minute or two, obscuring the prim Victorian dining-room and its familiar contents—a mist through which the three lit gas-globes on the brass chandelier shone large, round, and haloed like sun-dogs in the Far North.

The mist, clearing, left everything distinct again. The thundering voice subsided again to its former dry monotone. The lawyer brought his reading to a close, folded his eyeglasses, and replaced his documents in his bag. A discreet murmur of excited talk broke out among the relatives.

The dyspeptic niece, important in the consciousness of her legacy, came twittering up to Broughton as he rose to go.

"*So* kind of you to come, Captain Broughton! My uncle would have appreciated your being here. And you'll let me know where to send your picture, won't you? I'm so glad it's going to you. One likes to think things are going to those who will appreciate them."

The picture! Broughton nearly laughed in the woman's face—nearly told her to keep the damned picture. But he thought better of it—it wasn't the poor silly creature's fault, after all!

The lawyer hailed him as he stood on the steps, buttoning his overcoat, while he waited for his hansom.

"Can't I give you a lift anywhere, Captain Broughton? Going to be a foggy night, I fancy."

Broughton shook his head with a curt "No, thanks—walking!"

The little lawyer, who was a shrewd observer of men and, like most chatterboxes, a kindly soul, and who was, moreover, none too pleased with his own legacy, shook his head and sighed as he watched the square-set figure disappear into the fog and darkness.

"That man's had a bit of a knock," he reflected. "Wonder if he's got anything to live on? Not much, I dare say. Wouldn't have hurt that stingy old devil to leave him a hundred or two.... Ah well...."

V

Broughton strode away through the foggy suburban streets. He was afraid he'd been a bit offhand with that lawyer chap. Well, he couldn't help that! He felt he couldn't stand his gabble—not at present.

He wanted above everything else to be alone. He didn't feel as if he could face the well-meant curiosity and the equally well-meant sympathy of those men who had wished him luck that morning. His wound had struck too deep for such superficial salves to be other than an added irritation. Normally inclined to err on the side of amiability, he felt just now at odds with all the rest of humankind. He could fancy the whispers that would follow him—"There goes poor Broughton—feeling pretty sickish, you bet!"

The first staggering sensation of blank and bewildered disappointment had passed away, and in its place there surged up within him a cold tide of black anger against Old Featherstone.

So the old devil had been laughing at him in his sleeve that night—even as he was laughing at him now, very likely, in whatever unholy place he was gone to! He had guessed his thoughts, he supposed, in that damned uncanny way he had. If the dead face now lying under the cold cemetery mould had lain in Broughton's pathway now he would have ground his heel into the sardonic smile that still curled its stiff and silent lips.

Him and his blasted picture!... A thing that wasn't worth giving wall-space to! A damned ship-chandler's daub! Why, give him a few splashes of ship's paint and a brush and he'd make a better fist at it himself!

He strode blindly on, through interminable crescents of smug villas, their pavements greasy with fallen leaves, along dreary streets of shabby "semis," without noticing or caring where he was going: swinging his neatly rolled umbrella regardless of the fine rain which had begun to fall and was gathering in a million glistening drops on his black coat. His mood cried aloud for the relief of physical effort, of physical discomfort. Now and then he was brought up short by a blank wall that drove him back upon his traces; now and then he cannoned unnoticing into passing pedestrians, who turned, conscious of something unusual in his manner, to watch him out of sight, then continued their way wondering if he were drunk or mad.

Presently the streets of dull "semis" gave place to streets of seedy rows, with here and there a corner off-licence or a fried-fish shop discharging its warm oily odours upon the chill air; and at last, turning a corner, he found himself suddenly in a wide road whose greasy pavements were lined with stalls and flares, yelling salesmen, and groups of draggle-tailed women.

He looked about him stupidly, uncertain of his bearings, though the blare of a ship's syren striking on his ear told him that he was not far from the river. He was suddenly aware that he was wet and hungry and very tired, and that his feet in his best boots hurt him abominably, for he was no better a walker than most sailormen. He asked a passing pedestrian where he was.

"Lower Road, Deptford."... Why, he was less than a quarter of an hour's walk from the Surrey Commercial Docks, where the "Maid of Athens" was even now lying, having just finished discharging the cargo of linseed she had loaded at the River Plate. He couldn't do better than get on to the ship, he decided; he had been knocked out of time, and no mistake, and there he would be able to sit down quietly and think things over.

The fog, which had been comparatively light on the higher ground, had been steadily growing denser as he neared the river. There were haloes round the flares that roared above the street stalls, and the lighted shop windows were mere luminous blurs in the surrounding murk.

"Want to mind where you're steppin' to-night, Cap'n," the watchman hailed him as he passed the dock gates; "it's thick, an' no mistake—thick as ever I see it!"

Thick wasn't the word for it! Once away from the fights and noise of the road, the darkness seemed like something you could feel—a solid mass of clammy, clinging moisture, catching at the throat like a cold hand, getting into the backs of your eyes and making them ache and smart. You couldn't see your hand before your face.

Broughton groped his way along the narrow, slimy causeway which lay between the stacks of piled-up lumber, exuding their sharp, damp, resinous fragrance, and the intense darkness, broken occasionally by a vague tremulous reflection where some ship's lights contrived to pierce it, which brooded over the unseen waters of the dock. Lights showed forlornly here and there at the openings of the lanes which led away between the piled deals—abysses of blackness as dark as the Magellanic nebulæ. Ship's portholes gleamed round and watchful as the eyes of huge monsters of the slime. Bollards started up suddenly out of the fog like menacing figures, and cranes straddled the path like black Apollyons in some marine Pilgrim's Progress. Once Broughton pulled himself up only just in time to save himself from stepping over the edge of a yawning pit of nothingness in which the water lipped unseen against the slimy piles. The thought involuntarily crossed his mind that perhaps he might have done worse; but he put it from him resolutely. His code, a simple one, did not admit suicide as a permissible solution of the problems of life.

All work was long since over, and the docks were as silent and deserted as the grave—nothing to be heard but the steady drip-drip of the rain, once the distant tinkle of a banjo on board some vessel out in the dock, and now and again the melancholy wail of a steamer groping her way up river. The "Maid of Athens" lay right at the far end of one of the older basins; she was all still and dark but for the oil lamp that burned smokily at the head of the gangway, and a faint glow from the galley which showed where the old shipkeeper sat alone with his pipe and his memories.

Old Mike came hobbling out at the sound of Broughton's step on the plank.

"'Strewth, Cap'n," he exclaimed in astonishment, "you've chose a grand night to come down an' no fatal error! Will I make a bit o' fire in the cabin an' brew ye a cup o' tea? Sure you're wet to the skin!"

"Poor old chap!" Broughton thought, as he watched him busying himself about his fire-lighting with the gnarled and shaking hands that had hauled on so many a tackle-fall in their day. It would be a hard blow for him when he knew that ship was to be sold. He had served in Featherstone's ships many years as A.B. and latterly as bos'n, until a fall from aloft put an end to his seagoing days; and this little job of shipkeeping was one of the very few planks between him and the workhouse.

The world was none too kind to old men who had outlived their usefulness. What was it that old flintstone had said: "You can't teach an old dog new tricks"? Well, that was true enough, anyway!

He called to mind an incident that had happened in Sydney his last voyage there. An old man had come up to him begging for a job. He didn't care what—night watchman, anything; and he had opened his coat to show that he had neither waistcoat nor shirt beneath it.

"You don't remember me, Broughton," the old fellow had said; and, looking closer, he had recognized in that incredibly seedy wreck one of his own old skippers—before whose almost godlike aloofness and majesty he had once trembled in mingled fear and awe. It was a pitiful tale he had to tell. He had been thrown out of a berth at sixty-five, through his ship being lost by no fault of his own, and couldn't get in anywhere. That proud, arrogant old man, full of small vanities!... Broughton had had little enough cause in the past to think of him over kindly; but the memory of the encounter had remained with him for weeks at the time, and returned to trouble him now with an added significance.

Old Mike's bit o' fire smouldered a little and went out, leaving nothing but an acrid stink to mark its passing. The well-stewed tea in the enamel cup at his elbow, with the two ragged slices of margarine-plastered bread beside it in the slopped saucer, grew cold unheeded. Outside, the rain dripped down like slow tears. And there he sat, with his clenched hands before him on the table, staring into the Past.

There wasn't a plank of her, not a rivet, not a rope-yarn that didn't mean something to him. True, Old Featherstone had given his money for her: and if he knew that old man aright he hadn't given a brass farthing more than he could help. But he—what had he given to her? Money—well, he had given that, too, since Old Featherstone had turned mean, though his twenty pounds a month hadn't run to a great deal. But that was neither here nor there. Things money could never buy he was thinking of, sitting there in the cold, fog-dimmed cabin.

The years of his life had gone into her—affection, understanding, ungrudging service, sleepless nights and anxious days. What wonder that she seemed almost like a part of himself? What wonder that to a man of his rigid, slow-moving type of mind a future in which she had no part was a thing unthinkable?

His memory passed on to all the mates and second mates who had faced him at meals over that very cabin. A regular procession of them—Marston—Reid—what was the name of that chap with the light eyelashes?—Barnes, was it?—Digby—he was a decent chap, now—went into steam years ago and was chief officer in one of the B. I. ships last time Broughton heard of him. That was what *he* ought to have done. He had known it at the back of his mind all along. But he couldn't leave her—he couldn't leave her!

Well, well, there was no use meeting trouble half-way! What was it old Waterhouse, his first skipper in his brassbound days, used to say? "If you're jammed on a lee shore and can't stay, why, then try wearing. If that don't work, try boxing her off. But whatever you do, do something! Don't sit down and howl!"

They used to laugh at him and mimic him behind his back, cheeky young devils; but it was damned good advice for all that. He was on a lee shore now right enough; but there was bound to be a way out somewhere if he kept his head.

An intense drowsiness and weariness had begun to creep over him—just such a leaden desire for sleep as he had experienced in that same cabin many a time after days of incessant and anxious battling with gales and seas. His unmade bed looked singularly unenticing, so, dragging a blanket from the pile upon it, he kicked off his sodden boots and lay down on the cabin settee.

A rising wind had begun to moan and sigh in the rigging, driving the rain in sheets against the skylight ... there was a way out, a way out ... if he could only think of it ... somewhere....

VI

He awoke to a flood of bright sunshine streaming in through the skylight. The wind had driven fog and rain before it, leaving a virginal and new-washed world under a sky of pale, remote blue.

Broughton heaved himself off the settee, catching a glimpse of himself—haggard, rumpled, and unkempt—in the mirror over the sideboard, as he did so.

"By George!" he said to himself, viewing his reflection, "Marianne would have looked down her nose at me if I'd turned up at Sibella Road like this. She'd have thought I'd been having a thick night, and small blame to her!"

There was no doubt that he presented a sorry spectacle. His trousers were still damp and splashed with mud-stains; his collar was creased and black with fog. He was stiff and tired in body; but his mind, naturally resilient, was infinitely refreshed by the long hours of sleep.

His spirits rose every minute. He whistled to himself as he rummaged out a blue suit from his cabin, washed, and shaved. He even indulged in a smile as he recalled the little lawyer and his two singlets.

After all, looked at in the light of day, things might have been a whole lot worse. There was always a chance that one of the three or four British firms who still owned sailing ships might buy the old girl. She had a great name; and people were beginning to be a bit sentimental about sailing ships now they were mostly gone. Or one of the big steamship lines might take her on for training purposes. If either of those things happened, it wasn't likely they would want to put anyone else in command. It was common knowledge, though he said it himself, that no one could get what he could out of her. They would very likely put her into the nitrate trade. Of course it would be a bit of a come-down, still—any port in a storm! He remembered how sick he had been about it the first time she loaded coal at Newcastle. He had felt like going down on his knees and apologizing to her for the outrage! Or, again, there was lumber—plenty of charters were to be had up the West Coast. True, her size was against her; with her reputation and twice her tonnage she wouldn't have had to wait long for a purchaser. But she would be a good investment, for all that. Why, damn it all, if he had the money loose he'd buy her himself without thinking twice about it! But twenty pounds a month doesn't leave much margin for such luxuries as buying ships.

He paused half in and half out of his coat, struck by a sudden idea.

His half-brother Edward! Why, he was the very man—just the very man! Rolling in money that he made at that warehouse where he sold staylaces or something up in the City! The blighter was as sharp as a needle—always had been from the time when he used to drive bargains over blood alleys with the other kids at school. He'd see the advantage of a proposition like this fast enough! He could either lend the money on reasonable interest on the security of the ship, or if he liked he could buy her himself and let Broughton manage her for him.

He hurried over the rest of his toilet, swallowed a cup of tea and a rasher old Mike had got ready for him, and started off for the City, all on fire with his new project.

How did that piece of poetry go that Old Featherstone got the ship's name from? He had read it once, but he wasn't much at poetry: he couldn't make much of it.

"Maid of Athens, ere we part— —"

That was it! He repeated the line once or twice under his breath, finding in it a new and surprising significance. He ran his hand caressingly along the smoothness of her teak rail, sleek and glossy and warm in the sun as a living thing.

"Maid of Athens, ere we part— —"

"There's a deuce of a lot of water to go under the bridge before it comes to that, old lady!" he said aloud.

By the time he reached the dock gates the proposition had grown so rosy that his only fear was lest someone else should discover its attractiveness and get in ahead of him. By the time he got off the bus in Saint Paul's Churchyard it seemed to him that he was doing his half-brother a really good turn in allowing him the first chance of so advantageous a business opportunity.

The spruce-looking master mariner who gave in his name at a little hole marked "Inquiries" on the ground-floor of a warehouse just behind the Church of Saint Sempronius Without was a very different person from the haggard being who had glared back at him from the glass an hour ago.

Edward Broughton's place of business was a large, modern edifice each of whose many ground-floor windows displayed a device representing a nude youth running like hell over the surface of a miniature globe, holding in his extended hand a suit of Elasto Underwear—"Fits where it Hits." This famous slogan it was which had made Elasto Underwear and Edward Broughton's fortune; for he was by way of doing very well indeed, was Edward, and had even been spoken of as a possible Lord Mayor. David remembered him in the old days, when he was at home from sea, as a pert little snipe of a youngster with red cheeks and sticking-out eyes.

A stylish youth, looking like a clothed edition of the young gentleman on the placards, ushered him into a small, glass-sided compartment and left him alone there with two little plaster images wearing miniature suits of Elasto Underwear. One was after—a long way after—Michael Angelo's David, the other (also a long way) after the Venus of Milo.

Broughton looked round him with all the sailorman's lordly contempt of the ways of traders. He looked out through the glass sides of his cage on long vistas of desks where girls sat at typewriters and between which there scurried young exquisites with sleek hair and champagne-coloured socks—dozens of them, presumably engaged on the one all-important task of distributing Elasto Underwear to the civilized and uncivilized world.

So this was where brother Edward made all his money! Rum sort of show — "Fits where it Hits," indeed — what a darned silly idea! And how much longer were they going to keep him waiting?

His eyes wandered for the twentieth time to the clock. Half-past eleven — he had been here half an hour. The two underclothed statuettes were beginning to get on his nerves. He should smash 'em if he stopped there much longer.

Issuing forth fuming from his plate-glass seclusion, he stopped one of the hurrying exquisites.

"Does Mr. Broughton know I am here?" he asked.

"Y-yes, sir!" The youth could not have said what made him tack that "sir" on. "You see, he's very busy in a morning, if you haven't an appointment. And this week the auditors are here. Could you leave your name and call again?"

"I see. No, I'm afraid I can't. Will you have the goodness to tell him again, please? Say that Captain Broughton would like to see him — on business — important business."

The lad hesitated for a moment between dread of his employer and a sense of something masterful, something which demanded obedience, about this brown-faced, quiet stranger. The stranger won, and with a "Very good, sir," the messenger disappeared among the desks.

Presently he returned. Mr. Broughton would see his visitor now.

David's half-brother sat in a vast lighted room behind a vast leather-covered table. He still had the round red cheeks and prominent eyes of his youth, but he was almost bald and showed an incipient corporation.

A youth laden with two huge ledgers backed out of the presence as David entered. Like the King, by Jove! Brother Edward was getting into no end of a big pot.

"Oh, good morning, David!" He waved his caller graciously to a seat. "This is quite an unaccustomed honour. I'm afraid you've come at rather a busy time — the auditors, and so forth. I hardly ever see anybody except by appointment. But I can give you ten minutes. And now — what can I do for you?"

The words were pleasant enough in a way; but that "What can I do for you?" signified as plainly as if he had said it, "What does this fellow want with me, I wonder?"

There is no enmity so undying as that which dates from the nursery. There is no dislike so unconquerable as that which exists between people who are kin but not kind. Had David Broughton been more of a man of the world he would have known as much; and that while it is true that blood is thicker than water, it is also true that upon occasion it can be more bitter than gall.

The undercurrent of suspicion which was unmistakable beneath the smooth surface of Edward Broughton's words flicked David on the raw. Perhaps it was that, perhaps the long chilling wait in the plate-glass ante-room had something to do with it. For whatever reason, when he opened his mouth to explain his errand, he found that all his eloquence had deserted him.

He was going to make a mess of it: he knew it as soon as he began to speak. Where were all the telling facts, the effective data he had marshalled so brilliantly as he rode up to the City on the bus? Gone—all gone; he found himself stammering out his case haltingly, baldly, unconvincingly. He could feel it in his bones.

Edward Broughton pursed up his lips, as his half-brother's last phrase petered out in futility, and blew out his cheeks. He lay back in the large chair and spread his neat little legs out under the large table, placing together his finger-tips—the flattened finger-tips of the money-grubber.

"I—see! I—see! You want me to buy this—er—ship?"

"Well, yes," David admitted. "I suppose that's about the length of it, or—or—as I said just now—lend me the money on the security of the ship——"

Edward Broughton studied his nails for a few seconds in silence. He used to bite 'em as a kid, David suddenly remembered, and have bitter aloes put on to stop him.

Then slowly, solemnly, he shook his head.

"No, no! I'm afraid it's nothing in my line, David."

"But, dash it all, man!"—Broughton's temper was beginning to get the better of him. He was annoyed with himself because he felt he had bungled his chances: more because he felt that he had made a mistake in coming to this fellow at all. Ancient family aversions reared their forgotten heads. And the intolerant impatience of the autocrat rose in resentment of opposition. "Dash it all, man, it's a good investment! I shouldn't have thought about mentioning it to you if it hadn't been." He couldn't help that sly dig.

"What precisely is your idea of a good investment?"

"Well, I should say it would pay a good five per cent—at a low estimate...."

Edward raised his eyebrows with a superior little smile of indulgent amusement.

"Five per cent. Why, my dear man, I won't look at anything that doesn't bring in twenty at least. No, I'm very sorry for you. If I could really see my way to help you I would, for the sake of old times and so on. But one must keep sentiment out of business. It doesn't do. And, honestly, I can see nothing in it. It isn't even as if this ship were a fairly new ship. One must move with the times, you know. The late Mr. Featherstone was a very keen man of business, and as you yourself said just now, he'd been selling his ships for years. He knew his business, no doubt, as well as I know mine. And my motto is, 'Let the cobbler stick to his last!' His Elasto, eh? Ha ha— not bad that!... No, I'm awfully sorry! I quite see your position. I've often thought you were making a big mistake—you ought to have gone in with one of the steamer companies. But I'll do what I can for you. I'll put in a word for you, with pleasure. I know one or two directors——"

"Sorry! Help you! Put in a word for you!" What did the little blighter mean? A little snipe whose ear-hole he'd wrung many a time!

Broughton rose, breathing heavily. He restrained with difficulty a fraternal impulse to reach across the leather-covered table and pull the little beggar's nose.

"Damn it all," he rapped out, "who asked you for your pity or your advice, I'd like to know? When I want 'em, I won't forget to ask for 'em, and that'll be never. I come to you, as I might go to any other business man, with a business proposition. It doesn't interest you; very well, there's no more to be said. But as for your advice—*and* your money—you can keep 'em and be damned to you!"

He passed out between the lines of sniggering, nudging, whispering clerks, his head held high, though his heart was sick with anger and humiliation. So that was what the little beast had thought he was after. Keeping a berth warm for himself. He went hot all over at the thought. He did not even know that he had—for his voice, which he had raised considerably in the heat of the moment, had carried to the farthest corners of the outer office—provided the employees of Elasto, Limited, with one of the most enjoyable moments of their somewhat dull business career.

VII

The "Maid of Athens" left Northfleet six weeks later with a cargo of cement for British Columbia, where she was to load lumber for some port as yet unspecified, in accordance with a charter made before Old Featherstone's death.

The day had dawned grey and melancholy. A mist of fine, drizzling rain blotted out the low, monotonous shores of the estuary, and the crew—dull and dispirited, the last night's drink not yet out of them—hove the anchor short with hardly a pretence of a shanty. But a fresh, sharp wind began to blow from the north-east as the light grew, and presently the ship was romping down Channel with everything set.

Broughton stood on the poop beside the Channel pilot, watching the familiar coast of so many landfalls slip rapidly by. Like him, the red-faced, stocky man at his side had watched the ship grow old. His name figured many a time, in Broughton's stiff, precise handwriting, in those shabby, leather-backed volumes which recorded her unconsidered Odyssey:

> "6 a.m. Dull and rainy. Landed Mr. Gardiner, Channel pilot."

> "Start point bearing N. 6 miles. Pilot Gardiner left."

> "Off Dungeness, 3 a.m. Took Mr. Gardiner, pilot, off North Foreland."

Bald, unadorned entries, dull statements of plain fact set down by plain men with no knowledge of phrase-turning; yet there is more eloquence in them than in all the word-spinnings of literature to those who read aright. What sagas unsung they stand for! What departures fraught with hopes and dreams, with remorse and parting and farewell! What landfalls that were the triumphant climax of long endurance, of patient toil, of cold, hunger, heat, thirst, not to be told in words! What difficulties met and surmounted, what battles fought and won!

The ship glistened white and clean in the morning sun. The men were hard at work washing down decks, ridding her of the last traces of the grime accumulated during her long period in port. Ah, thought Broughton, it was good to be at sea again! The doubts and anxieties of the last six weeks seemed to slip away from him as the river mud slipped from the ship's keel into the clean Channel tide. The accustomed sights and sounds, the familiar lift and quiver of his ship under him, were like a kind of enchanted circle within which he stood secure against the dark forces of destruction and change. He was a king again in his own little kingdom. The very act of entering up the day's work in the log book—the taking of sights—all the small duties and ceremonies that make up a shipmaster's life—helped to create in him an illusion of security. He was like a man awakened from a terrifying dream of judgment, reassuring himself by the sight and touch of common things that the world still goes on its accustomed way. A strange sense of peace and permanency wrapped him round—the peace of an ancient and established order of things seeming so set and rooted that nothing could ever end it. It seemed incredible that all this microcosm should pass away—that the uncounted watches should ever go by and the ship's faithful bells tell them no more. She appeared to borrow a certain quality of immortality from the winds and the sea and the stars, the eternal things which had been the commonplaces of her wandering years.

Most of all, it was the fact of being once more occupied that brought him solace. By what queer doctrine of theologians, by what sheer translator's error, did man's inheritance of daily labour come to be accounted as the penalty of his first folly and sin? Work—surely the one merciful gift vouchsafed to Adam by an angry Deity when he went weeping forth from Paradise! Work—with its kindly weariness of body, compelling the weary brain to rest. Work, the everlasting anodyne, the unfailing salve for man's most unbearable sorrows—which shall last when pleasure and lust and wealth are so many Dead Sea apples in the mouth, a comfort and a refuge when all human loves and loyalties shall fade and fail.

Five days after the "Maid of Athens" took her departure from the Lizard it began to breeze up from the north-west. At three bells in the first watch the royals and topgallantsails had to come in, then the jibs; and when dark fell she was running before wind and sea under fore and main topsails and reefed foresail. But she liked rough weather, and under her reduced canvas she was going along very safely and easily, so Broughton decided to turn in for an hour's rest in order to be ready for the strenuous night he anticipated.

"I am going to turn in for an hour or so," he said, turning to the mate; "call me in that time, if I am not awake before. And sooner if anything out of the way should happen. I think we shall have a dirty night by the look of it."

The mate was a poor creature—weak, but with the self-assertiveness that generally goes with weakness. Broughton felt he would not like to rely upon him in an emergency.

But he had had very little sleep since the ship sailed—nor, indeed, during the weeks which had elapsed since Featherstone's funeral. He shrank instinctively from being alone. It was then that his anxieties began to crowd upon him afresh, and that the threat of the future seemed to touch him like the shadow of some boding wing. But now that sudden overpowering heaviness of the eyelids which must inevitably, sooner or later, follow upon a continued sleeplessness, descended upon him. He felt that he could hardly keep awake—no, not though the very skies should fall.

He was sound asleep almost as soon as he had lain down—lost in a labyrinth of ridiculous and confusing dreams in which all sorts of unexpected people and events kept melting into one another in the most illogical and inconsequent fashion, which yet seemed, according to that peculiar fourth-dimensional standard of values which prevails in the dream-world, perfectly proper and reasonable.

Old Featherstone figured in these dreams: so also did the dining-room at "Pulo Way." Only somehow Old Featherstone kept turning into somebody else; first it was Hobbs the lawyer, then old Mike Brophy the shipkeeper, then an old mate of his called Peters, whom he hadn't seen or thought of even for years. And then the dining-room had become the cabin of the "Maid of Athens," and Peters, who had changed into old Captain Waterhouse, was sitting at the head of the table reading Featherstone's will. He was shouting at the top of his voice, and Broughton was straining his ears to catch what he was saying and couldn't make out a word of it because of the roar of the wind. And then the floor began to heave and slant, and the pictures on the walls—for the cabin had turned back into a dining-room again—to tumble all about his ears—and the next moment he was sitting up broad awake, his feet and back braced to meet the next lurch of the vessel, the wind and sea making a continuous thunder outside, and a pile of books cascading down upon him from a shelf over his head.

He knew well enough—his seaman's instinct told him almost before he was fully awake—precisely what had happened. It was just the very possibility which had been in his mind when he turned in. The mate—aided no doubt by a timorous and inefficient helmsman—had let the ship's head run up into the wind and she had promptly broached to. The "Maid" always carried a good deal of weather helm, and wanted careful watching with a following wind and sea. He remembered an incident which had occurred years ago, while he was running down the Easting—a bad helmsman had lost his head through watching the following seas instead of his course, and let the ship run away with him. Broughton had been close to him when it happened. He struck the man a blow that sent him rolling in the scuppers, and himself seized the spokes and jammed the helm up. The mate, in the meantime, had let the topsail halyards run without waiting for the order, and, freed from the weight of her canvas, the ship paid off and the danger was over.

The memory flashed through his mind and was gone during the few seconds it took him to grope his way to the door and emerge into the roaring, thundering darkness beyond.

The ship lay sprawled in the trough of the sea, like a horse fallen at a fence. Her lee rail was buried four feet deep, and her lower yards were hidden almost to the slings in the seething, churned-up whiteness which surrounded her. The night was black as pitch. A pale glimmer showed faintly from the binnacle, and the sickly red and green of the side-lights gleamed wan and fitful amid the watery desolation. But otherwise the only fight was that which seemed to be given by the white crests of the endless procession of galloping seas which came tearing out of the night to pour themselves over the helpless vessel.

The wheel appeared to be still intact; in the darkness Broughton thought he could still make out the hunched figure of the helmsman beside it. That was so much. If the spars held....

As he emerged from the shelter of the chart-room the full force of the wind struck him like a steady push from some huge, invisible hand. He waited for a lull and made a dash for the wheel.

The lull was for a few moments only—a few moments during which the ship lay in the lee of a tremendous sea, which, towering up fifty feet above her, held her for a brief space in its perilous and betraying shelter. The next instant it broke clean over her—a great mass of green marbled water that filled her decks, carried her boats away like matchboxes down a flooded gutter, and swept her decks from end to end with a triumphant trampling as of a conquering army.

"This finishes it!" Broughton thought.

He was swept clean off his feet; rolled over and over; buried in foam; engulfed in what seemed to him like the whole Atlantic ocean; carried, as he believed, right down to Davy Jones's locker, where the light of day would never reach him again....

The next thing he knew he was lying jammed against the lee rail of the poop, his legs hanging outboard, his arm hooked round a cleat, presumably by some subconscious instinct of self-preservation, for he had no recollection of putting it there. The water was pouring past him in a green cataract, and dragging at him like clutching fingers. He was alive. The ship was alive. "Good old girl!" Broughton said to himself. He began to struggle to his feet. Something moved beside him and clawed at his ankles.

"Oh, Lord!" said a voice out of the darkness—the mate's voice. "Oh, Lord—I thought I was a goner!"

"Oh—you!" said Broughton. "Get off my feet, damn you!"

"Oh, Lord!" said the voice again.

"Pull yourself together!" Broughton rapped out. "What were you doing? Why didn't you call me?"

"There wasn't time," moaned the mate. "She was going along all right, and the next minute—oh, Lord, I was nearly overboard!"

"Think you're at a bloody revival meeting?" snapped Broughton. He shook him off, and, holding by the rail, fought his way up the slanting deck to the wheel.

The young second mate came butting head down through the murk.

"Fore upper topsail's gone out of the bolt-ropes, sir!"

Broughton smiled grimly to himself. Old Featherstone's skinflint ways had turned out good policy for once. If that fore upper topsail had held, as it would have done if it had been the stout Number One canvas his soul craved, instead of a flimsy patched affair only fit for the Tropics, they might all have been with Davy Jones by now.

"Take the best hands you can find to the braces," Broughton ordered. "I must try to get her away before it. Mister!"—this to the mate, who had by this time picked himself out of the scuppers and came scrambling up the deck—"take half a dozen hands down to see to the cargo, and do what you can to secure it if it looks like shifting."

The helmsman, a big heavy Swede, was still clinging to the wheel like a limpet; partly because it appeared to him good to have something to hold on to, partly because his wits worked so slowly that it hadn't yet occurred to him to let go. Broughton grasped the spokes and the two men threw every ounce of their strength into the task of putting the helm over.

Gusts of cheery obscenity came out of the darkness forward as the crew fought to get the spars round. "Good men!" Broughton said between his teeth. "'Maid of Athens, ere we part,' eh? Not yet, old girl—not yet!"

It seemed as if the helpless ship knew the feel of the familiar hand on her helm, and strove with all her might to respond to it. She struggled; she almost rose. Then, wind and sea beating her down anew, she slid down into the trough again.

Again and again she tried to heave herself free from the weight of water that dragged her down; again and again she slipped back again, like a fallen horse trying vainly to get a footing on a slippery road. The two men wrestled with the wheel in grim silence. It kicked and strove in their grasp like a living thing. But at last, slowly, the ship quivered, righted herself. She shook the seas impatiently from her flanks as the reefed foresail filled. Inch by inch the yards came round to windward. The fight was over.

By daybreak the gale had all but blown itself out. The sea still ran high, but the wind had fallen, and a watery sun was trying to break through the hurrying clouds. The hands were already at work bending a new foretopsail, and their short, staccato cries came on the wind like the mewings of gulls.

"Life in the old dog yet, Mr. Kennedy!" said Broughton to the second mate. He struck his hands together, exulting. The struggle seemed to him a good omen. If she could live through a night like that, surely she could also survive those obscurer dangers which threatened her. His shoulders ached like the shoulders of Atlas from the battle with the kicking wheel. He had not known such physical effort since his apprentice days. The fight had put new heart into him. By God, it had been worth it, he told himself. It made a man feel that it was worth while to be alive....

A few days later the "Maid of Athens" picked up the north-east Trades, and carried them with her almost down to the Line through a succession of golden days and star-dusted nights. She loitered through the doldrums—found her Trades again just south of the Line—wrestled with the Westerlies off the Horn—and, speeding northward again through the flying-fish weather, made the Strait of Juan de Fuca a hundred and nine days out.

VIII

The "Maid of Athens" discharged her cargo of cement at Vancouver, and went over to the Puget Sound wharf at Victoria to load lumber for Chile.

She was there for nearly a month before she left her berth on a fine October afternoon, and anchored in the Royal Roads, where the pilot would board her next morning to take her down to Flattery.

Broughton went ashore in the evening for the last time, and walked up to his agent's offices in Wharf Street. He was burningly anxious to be at sea again. The old restlessness was strong upon him that he had felt before leaving London River, and a number of small vexatious delays had whetted his impatience to the breaking point.

"Letter for you, Cap'n," the clerk hailed him. "I thought maybe you'd be around, or I'd have sent it over to you."

Broughton turned the letter in his hands for a minute or two before opening it. He recognized the prim, clerkly hand at once. It was from

Jenkinson. A cold wave of apprehension flooded over him. Some mysterious kind of telepathy told him that it contained unwelcome tidings.

He slit the envelope at last, unfolded the sheet, and read it through. Then he read it again, and still again—uncomprehendingly, as if it were something in a foreign and unknown language:

" ...Sorry to say the old ship has now been sold ... firm at Gibraltar ... understand she is to be converted into a coal hulk...."

Broughton crumpled the sheet in his hand with a fierce gesture, staring out with unseeing eyes into a world aglow with the glory of sunset. It was the worst—the very worst—he had ever dreamed of! Why hadn't he let her go, he wondered, that night in the North Atlantic? Why had he dragged her back from a decent death for a fate like this? He could have stuck it if she had gone to the shipbreakers. It would have hurt like hell, but he could have stuck it. But this; it made him think, somehow, of those old pitiful horses you saw being shipped across to Belgium with their bones sticking through their skins. People used to have their old horses shot when they were past work. They were different now. It was all money—money—money! They thought nothing of fidelity, of loyalty, of long service. They cared no more for their ships than for so many slop pails....

Wasn't it the old Vikings that used to take their old ships out to sea and burn them? There was a fine end for a ship now—a fine, clean, splendid death for a ship that had been a great ship in her day! He remembered once, years ago, watching a ship burn to the water's edge in the Indian Ocean. He wasn't much more than a nipper at the time, but he had never forgotten it. The calm night, and the stars, and the ship flaring up to heaven like a torch. He didn't think he would have minded, somehow, seeing his old ship go like that. But this—oh, he had got to find a way out of it somehow....

"Bad news, Cap'n?" came the clerk's inquiring voice.

Broughton pulled himself together with an effort.

"No, no, thanks!" Mechanically he made his adieux and passed out into the street. He didn't know where he was going. He never remembered how he found his way to the Outer Wharf where his boat was waiting.

But he must have got there somehow, for now he was sitting in the stern-sheets and looking out across the water to the ship lying at anchor, with eyes to which sorrow and the shadow of parting seemed to have given a strange new apprehension of beauty. How lovely she looked, he thought, with the little pink clouds seeming to be caught in her rigging, and the gulls flying and calling all about her! It was queer that he should notice things like that so much, now that he was going to lose her. He had known the time when he would have taken it all for granted. Now, he kept seeing all kinds of little things in a kind of new, clear light, as if he saw them for the first time— —

Let young Kennedy tell the rest of the tale—in his cabin in a Blue Funnel liner, years afterwards; the unforgettable, indefinable smell of China drifting up from the Chinese emigrants' quarters, the gabble of the stokers at their interminable fan-tan on the forecastle mingling with the piping of the gulls along the wharf sheds.

"I could see at once" (thus young Kennedy) "that something had gone wrong with the Old Man. He looked ten years older since I had seen him a couple of hours before. He came up the ladder very slowly and heavily, passed me by without speaking—I might have been a stanchion standing there for all the notice he took of me—and went down into the cabin almost as if he were walking in his sleep.

"Something—I don't exactly know what—intuition, perhaps, you'd call it—made me trump up an excuse to follow him. I didn't like the looks of him, somehow.

"I found him sitting in his chair by the table, staring straight before him with that same fixed look as if he didn't really see anything.

"He didn't so much as turn his head when I went in, and at first when I spoke he didn't seem to hear me. I spoke again, a little louder, and he gave a sort of start, as if he had been suddenly roused out of a sleep.

"'Yes—no!' he said in a dazed kind of way. 'Yes—no' (like that); and then suddenly, in a very loud, harsh voice, quite different from his ordinary way of speaking: 'A hulk! A hulk! They are going to make a coal hulk of her!'

"The words seemed to be fairly ripped out of him. He didn't seem to be speaking to me. It was more as if he were trying to make himself believe something that was too bad to realize.

"I managed to say something—I forget just what: that it was rotten luck, perhaps. I doubt if he heard me, anyhow, for he went on in the same strange voice, like someone talking to himself.

"'She's good for twenty years yet!' And then, in a sort of choking voice, 'Mine—mine, by God, mine!'

"Well, I just turned at that and bolted. I felt I couldn't stand any more. It seemed like eavesdropping on a man's soul.

"I didn't see him again until the next morning, when the tug came alongside as soon as it was light. He came on deck looking as if nothing had happened. I never said anything, of course—no more did he; and from that day to this I don't really know—though I rather fancy he did—if he remembered what had passed between us.

"We had a fine passage down to Iquique, where we discharged our lumber and loaded nitrates for the U.K. The Old Man had got very fussy about the ship. He had every inch of her teak scraped and oiled while we were running down the Trades, and everything made as smart as could be aloft; and while we were lying at Iquique he had her figurehead, which was a very pretty one, all done over—pure white, of course. I did the best part of it myself, for I used to be reckoned rather a swell in the slap-dab business in those days, though I say it myself!

"Well, we finished our loading and left, and all the ships cheered us down the tier; and I don't wonder, for the old ship looked a picture.

"The Old Man and I had got to be quite friends. I suppose we were as near being pals as a skipper and a second mate ever could be. He was working on a new rail for the poop ladder—all fancy ropework and so on—and he used to bring it up on deck and yarn away to me about old times hour by the length. I fancy he rather liked me, but up till then he had always had a kind of stand-offish, you-keep-your-place-young-man way with him; and for my part I'd always looked on him with that sort of mixture of holy awe when he was there and disrespect behind his back a fellow has for the skipper he's served his time under. I suppose our both thinking such a lot of the old barky gave us an interest in common. You see, I'd served my time in her right from the start, so that naturally she was the ship of all ships for me—still is, for the matter of that.... Say what you will, she was a great old ship, and he was a great old skipper!"

(Kennedy paused. A quiver had crept somehow into his voice, and he had to get it under control again.)

"The Old Man" (he went on) "had always been what I should call a careful skipper. Not nervous—nothing of that sort—but cautious; I never knew him lose a sail but once, and never a spar. In fact, I used to feel a bit annoyed with him sometimes because he didn't go out of his way to take risks. He was a fine seaman; but there's no denying the fact he *was* cautious. He made some fine passages in the 'Maid of Athens,' and never a bad one. But he didn't really drive her. I believe he was too damned fond of her.

"So that you may imagine it was a bit of a surprise when we began to get into the high south latitudes and he started to crack on in a way that made even me open my eyes a little.

"I well remember the first day I noticed it. It was just on sunset—a black and red sort of affair with lots of low-hanging clouds, and the seas came rolling up with that ugly, sickly green on them when the light caught them that always goes with bad weather.

"It had been blowing pretty hard all day, and the glass dropping fast. The ship was labouring heavily and shipping quantities of water; she was loaded nearly to her marks with nitrates. There stood the skipper—I can just see him now—with his feet planted wide, holding on to the weather rigging and looking up aloft, as his way always was when it was blowing up.

"I expected him, of course, to order some of the canvas off her, for she was carrying a fairish amount considering the weather. So I was fairly taken aback, as you may imagine, when he turned round and said quite quietly:

"'I want the fore upper topsail reefed and set, Mr. Kennedy.'

"I was so surprised that I just stood and gaped for a minute or so. He looked at me in a sort of a challenging way, and said:

"'Didn't you hear the order? What are you waiting for?'

"I pulled myself together, said 'Fore upper topsail it is, sir!' and off I went. And I can tell you that for the next half hour or so I had plenty to occupy me without worrying my head about what the Old Man was thinking of.

"Well, we got the sail reefed and set. By this time the ship was ripping along at a good sixteen knots or more. You could see her wake spread out a mile behind her like a winding sheet. It was quite dark by this time. Her lee rail was right under, and making our way aft was like going through a swimming-bath.

"The Old Man was still standing just as I had left him, holding on with both hands to the weather rigging, and bracing his feet against the slant of the deck. I had hardly got my foot on the poop ladder when he turned his head and called to me. I could see his lips move, but I could hear nothing for the noise of the wind and sea.

"'Beg pardon, sir,' I yelled into the din.

"This time I managed to catch a word or two, but I could make nothing of it. It sounded like topgallantsails, but in spite of what had just happened I couldn't believe my own ears.

"'Are you deaf, or what's the matter with you?' yells the Old Man then. 'That's twice I've had occasion to repeat an order. Don't let it occur again!'

"Well, off I struggled again forrard! 'What price Bully Forbes of the "Marco Polo,"' says I to myself; and I tried to fancy the old B.O.T. examiner's face that passed me for second, if I'd answered his pet question, 'Running before a gale, what would you do?' with 'Cram on more sail and chance it!'

"It took us a good ten minutes to make our way through the broken water on deck. We'd struggle forward a few yards, then—flop!—would come a big green one over the rail and send us all jumping for our lives—on again, and over would come another; still we got there at last, and after a bit we managed to set the sail. Then came the big tussle, at the braces up to our necks in water! More than once I thought we were all gone; but at last everything was O.K., gear turned up and all, and we hung on to windward as well as we could and put up a silent prayer—at least I know I did—that the Old Man wouldn't take it into his head to fly any more kites just yet.

"I'd always rather envied the fellows who were at sea twenty years or so before my time—the chaps who had such wonderful yarns to tell about the dare-devil skippers and the incredible cracking on in the China tea ships and the big American clippers. Well, I don't mind owning I was getting all of it I wanted for once!

"Mind you, it didn't worry me any! On the whole, I liked it. I was a youngster, with no best girl or anything of that sort to trouble about, and I enjoyed it. There was something so wonderfully fine and exciting in the feel of the thing, even when you knew at the back of your mind that she might go to glory any minute and take the whole blessed shooting-match along with her. But there wasn't much time to worry about details like that; and anyhow, after a certain point you just get beyond thinking about them one way or the other. It's all in the day's work, and there you are!

"But our precious mate, I must tell you, didn't like it a bit—not a little bit! He was a fellow called Arnot, rather a poisonous little bounder; I guess he'd none too much nerve to start with, and he'd played the dickens with what he had while we were in Iquique, running after what he called "skirts" and soaking *aguardiente*. The skipper's carrying on got on his nerves frightfully. He was scared stiff. He went about dropping dark hints about barratry, and chucking the ship away, and *he* wasn't the man to hold his tongue if he ever got back to England, and so on. He used to buttonhole me whenever we met and start burbling away about the Old Man being out of his mind.

"I ran bung into him one day as I came out of my room. It was blowing like the dickens and the ship tearing along hell-for-leather. I won't say what sail she was carrying, because I don't want to get the name of being a liar.

She was a wonderful old ship to steer (I hardly ever knew her need a lee wheel) or she could never have kept going as she did under all that canvas. If she'd once got off her course it would have been God help her!

"Mister Mate and I did one or two impromptu dance steps in each other's arms before we got straightened up again. I noticed two things about him while we were thus engaged. One was that by the smell of him he'd been imbibing a drop of Dutch courage from a private store I suspected he kept in his room—the other that he was fairly shaking with fright.

"'I s-s-say, you know, th-this is awful! He's—he's m-m-mad,' he stuttered. You really couldn't help feeling sorry for the little beast in a way. I believe he was nearly crying!

"'Mad nothing!' I said. 'Anyway, mad or sane, he knows a damn sight more about seamanship than either of us.' I'd a good mind to add that so far as he was concerned that wasn't saying much.

"Arnot moaned, 'He'll drown us all, that's what he'll do!' gave a despairing little flop with his arms, and dived into his room, for all the world like a startled penguin.

"I jolly well wasn't going to take sides against the skipper with a little squirt like Arnot, but in my own mind I was far from happy about him.

"What *was* he driving at? God knows!... Sometimes I think one thing, sometimes another. Was he trying to throw his ship away after all those years of command? I can't say. I know I knocked a couple of Mister Arnot's teeth into the back of his head for saying so, after it was all over; but that was more a matter of principle, and by way of relieving my feelings, than anything else. It looked like it, I must own. And yet I don't think it was quite that. It was more, if you understand me, that he just felt as if things had gone too far for him—so he threw his cards on the table, and left it to—well, shall we say Providence to shuffle them!

"Well, Mister Mate was going to have worse to put up with yet!

"The big blow lasted off and on for four days, and then it began to ease off a bit. I went below for a sleep: I was fairly coopered out. I just flopped down in my wet clothes and was off at once.

"When I came on deck again for the middle watch we were right in the thick of a dense white fog. There was a cold wind blowing steadily out of nowhere, and the ship was still going along, as near as I could judge, at about thirteen or fourteen knots. The first person I saw was the old bos'n—a Dutchman, and a real good sailorman, though a bit on the slow side, like most Dutchmen—standing under the break of the poop with his nose thrown up to windward, sniffing like an old dog.

"'Ice!' he said. 'I schmell ice!'

"I should think he did 'schmell' it! Phoo! but it was cold! The sails were like boards—as stiff and as hard. I doubt if we could have furled them if we had wanted to. The helmsman, when the wheel was relieved, left the skin of his fingers on the spokes. It was a queer, uncanny experience ... the ship ripping along through that blanket of fog, as tall and white as the ghost of a ship.... If there had been anyone else to see her, they might have been excused for thinking they'd met the 'Flying Dutchman' a few thousand miles off his usual course.

"And ice—there was ice everywhere! It must have been all round us, though we never saw it, only, as the bos'n said, 'schmelt' it and heard it. Sometimes there would be the sound of the seas breaking along it for miles; sometimes there would be the weird noises—shrieks and groans—that the bergs make when they are 'calving'; now and then cracks like musketry fire—and in the midst of it all the penguins would make you jump out of your skin with calling out exactly like human voices.

"There the Old Man stood on the poop, the whole time, more like a frozen image than a man—his arms laid along the spanker boom, and his chin resting on them—for hours, never speaking or moving.

"I went up to him at last and begged him to lie down, promising to call him if anything happened. He seemed to wake out of a dream just as he had done that day in the cabin at Victoria. His breath had congealed and frozen his beard to his sleeve, and he had to give a regular tug to get it loose. And he had to tear his hand away from the iron of the spar and leave the skin behind.

"I got him a cup of coffee, and he drank it down, and then he lay down on the settee in the chart-room. He called me back as I was leaving him, as if he were going to say something. But he only said, 'Never mind—it is nothing,' and lay down again.

"I looked in on him when the mate relieved me at eight bells. He was still fast asleep, and it came over me all of a sudden how old and tired he looked. I didn't see any sense in waking him, so I tiptoed off and left him.

"When I woke at seven bells I could tell at once by the movement of the ship that she had much less way on her. I don't mind owning I was more than a little relieved. The Old Man's cracking on had begun to get on my nerves a bit since the fog had come on. It was so unusual there was something uncanny about it. I don't suppose I should have cared a cuss if he'd been one of your dare-devil, Hell-or-Melbourne, what-she-can't-carry-she-must-drag sort of blighters. But, being the man he was, that he should suddenly bust out like this—well, it staggered me. It was like one's favourite uncle going Fanti.

"What had really happened, as it turned out, was that Mister Mate had taken the bull by the horns, and shortened sail while the Old Man was safely out of the way. It was dead against his orders, and when the skipper came on deck, which he did just as I turned up, there was a rare to-do.

"I never saw a man in such a passion. He was white and shaking with anger. He went for Arnot in a regular fury. Was he master of his own ship, or was he not? and so on, and so on. And then Arnot, who had lost his head altogether, started bawling back at him about barratry and Board of Trade inquiries.

"'You damned insubordinate hound!' yells the Old Man. I could see the big veins swell up on his forehead. I thought he would have struck the mate.

"And then—something happened. There was a jar and a grinding crash forward, and we were all thrown sprawling in a heap on the deck.

"The ship had driven bows on into a berg nearly as big as a continent, and then slowly slid off again. Nobody was hurt. The men came tumbling out of the deckhouse where they berthed before you could look round. I don't suppose any of them was asleep, for every one was getting a bit jumpy since we had been among the ice.

"The first thing I saw when I picked myself up was Arnot crawling out of the scuppers with such a comical look of surprise that I had to laugh. Then I saw the Old Man—and the laugh died.

"I shall never forget his face—miserable and yet lifted up both at once, if you understand me, like old what's-his-name—you know—sacrificing his daughter. There he stood, on the break of the poop, quite calm and collected, seeing to the swinging out of the boats, and making sure that they had food and water. Then at the last he went back to the chart-room to fetch the ship's papers.

"He sighed once, and looked round—a long look as if he were saying good-bye to it all in his heart. He let his hand rest on her rail for a minute, and I saw his lips move as if he were speaking to himself. Then he sighed again, and went in.

"The ship settled down very fast. We waited five minutes—ten minutes. I began to feel uneasy and went along to see what was detaining him. I glanced into the chart-room. He was sitting by the table: I could see his grey head—the hair getting a bit thin on top—just as I'd seen it scores of times. Nothing wrong that I could see....

"Fifteen minutes—twenty—I shoved my head in to tell him the boat was waiting....

"But I never got him told.... He must have had some sort of a stroke—evidently when he was going to make a last entry in the log, for the book lay open before him. I wonder what he was going to write in it. I wonder! Ah, well, no one will ever know that but his Maker.

"He was still breathing when we got him into the boat, but it was plain to see that no Board of Trade inquiry would ever trouble him.

"We only just pulled away from the ship in time. She went down quite steadily, on a perfectly even keel. I suppose her cargo—she was loaded right down to her marks—helped to keep her upright. She just settled quietly down, with a little shiver now and then like a person stepping into cold water. Her sails kept her up a little until they were soaked through. She looked—oh, frightfully like a drowning woman! The fog shut down like a curtain just at the finish, and the last I saw of her was like a white drowning hand thrown up out of the water. I was glad from my heart the Old Man couldn't see her. It was bad enough for me—a young fellow with all the world before me. I tell you, the salt on my cheeks wasn't all sea water! What it would have been like for him — —

"He was dead by the time a steamer picked us up, twelve hours later, and we buried him the same day, not many miles from the place where the old 'Maid of Athens' went down.

"Somehow, I think he would have been pleased if he knew.... You see, he thought a lot of the old ship...."

THE END OF AN ARGUMENT

AGOOD solid point of difference is, on the whole, almost as satisfactory as an interest in common—which, in the case of Kavanagh, the mate, and Ferguson, the chief engineer, of the tramp steamer "Gairloch," was fortunate, since of the latter commodity they possessed none at all.

Kavanagh was by way of being particular about his appearance, and shaved before the six inches of mirror in his cramped little cabin as religiously as any brassbound officer of a crack liner.

Ferguson was hairy and unbrushed both by inclination and principle.

Kavanagh was neat in his attire.

Ferguson was at his happiest in a filthy boiler suit, and he had a trick of using a handful of engineroom waste where other men use a pocket handkerchief, which annoyed Kavanagh almost to the point of tears.

Kavanagh's whole soul revolted against the smelly, smutty little tub which was for the time being his floating home. It was ungrateful of him, certainly, for she had done him a good turn after a fashion. But he couldn't help it. He was a sail-trained man; and he had remained in sail, out of a sheer sense of beauty which was no less real for being entirely inarticulate, long after his own interests indicated that he should leave it. Then the company with which he had grown up sold the last of its fleet, and he had perforce to seek employment elsewhere. He found it at last, though only after many long and weary weeks of hanging about docks and shipping offices—found it as mate of the "Gairloch."

He sang the praises of sail without ceasing. And even so did Ferguson wax lyrical on the theme of the engines of the "Gairloch."

She might not, he admitted, be beautiful externally; but, man, she'd gran' guts in her! He would then soar into ecstatic and highly technical rhapsodies concerning those same internal essentials, the technicalities being further complicated by a copious use of his native Doric, and decorated freely with a certain adjective of a sanguinary nature of which he was inordinately fond.

The argument began something after this fashion:

The "Gairloch" had not long cleared Victoria Harbour, and was belching forth an Acheronian smudge from her shabby funnel, as she butted her ugly hull into the south-westerly swell, when she met a big four-masted barque coming in to Hastings Mill for a cargo of Pacific Coast lumber. It was a glorious morning—one of those bright, calm, virginal mornings that are an especial climatic product of that coast. Everything was bathed in a flood of clear, pale sunlight. The opaque green waters of the Strait gleamed and flashed in the sun, and, clear-cut as if they were no more than a dozen miles away, the snowy summits of the Oregon ranges stood out dazzling in their whiteness against the blue of the early morning sky.

The barque was a tall ship for those days, with royals at fore, main, and mizen, and her piled-up sails shone white as the distant ranges in the sunlight that caressed their swelling surfaces. The hands were just laying aloft to get the canvas off her, and as she surged by with a bone in her mouth, her wet bows and white figurehead flashing as she lifted on the swell, Kavanagh's heart ached anew with an unquenchable longing for sail. In his mind he followed the noble ship to her moorings, in fancy heard the familiar nasal chant as sail after sail was furled:

> "We'll roll up the bunt with a fling—o—oh ...
> An' pa—ay Paddy Doyle for his bo—o—ots...."

"There's a ship for you!" he exclaimed to the wide world.

"Ah see nae beauty in yon," came a dour voice at his elbow—the voice of Ferguson. "Ah see nae beauty in thae bluidy windbags, nae mair than in ma wife's cla'es hingin' oot on the cla'es-line o' a Monday morning."

Kavanagh was annoyed. He had not meant his involuntary outburst of feeling to be overheard—least of all to be overheard by Ferguson. Sneaking about in carpet slippers....

"I dare say this floating abomination is more to your taste," he snapped.

"She's guid guts in her," said Ferguson.

The argument was still going on as merrily as ever while the "Gairloch" rolled heavily up from the Line through days which grew ever colder and winds which grew ever more stormy.

The little ship had struck the Western Ocean in one of the very worst of his moods. She was making shocking weather of it. She rolled, she pitched, she wallowed, she did every conceivable thing a deeply laden and ill-designed ship could do in a seaway. Her iron decks were most of the time under water, and the atmosphere of the stuffy little cabin, with every scuttle shut and the lamp smoking villainously as it swung in its gimbals, resembled that of the infernal regions.

But still, whenever Ferguson and Kavanagh met, the argument continued without abatement. They went on with it grimly, with their legs hooked on those of the cabin table, and their backs braced against the backs of their chairs, while, in spite of the fiddles that had graced the board for weeks, every roll of the ship added yet further contributions of cold potato and congealed meat to the dreary confusion of the cabin floor.

And so they might have gone on to the crack of doom had nothing happened to interrupt them.

In this case what happened was the sighting of the derelict.

It was about the end of the morning watch, one dark, dreary morning, when a late livid dawn was just creeping over the rim of the heaving waste of waters. Kavanagh was cold, tired, and depressed, and his reflections, as he stood on the bridge of the "Gairloch," were in harmony with the time and the weather. The future stretched before him no more cheerfully than that expanse of grey Atlantic—dreary, monotonous, and dismal to a degree. He didn't expect he would ever get a command. He ought to have gone into steam earlier. He might have got into one of the big liner companies. Now——

Precisely at this point in his meditations he sighted the deserted ship—now visible on the crest of a roller, now lost to sight as she slid drunkenly down into the trough of the sea.

It was evident at a glance that she was not under control. She was yawing helplessly hither and thither in the seas, her yards, with the rags of their sails still fluttering in the wind, pointing as if in mute appeal to the four quarters of the heavens.

"'Maria'—Genoa," said Kavanagh, with his glasses to his eyes, "and built on the Clyde by the looks of her.... I think she's been abandoned—I don't make out anyone moving, or any signal."

He handed the glasses to Captain Harrison, who had just come on to the bridge.

"Aye—she's derelict right enough," said the captain after a prolonged scrutiny. "Well, I'll have to report her—can't do anything more. It's out of the question taking a ship in tow in a sea like this."

He pulled at his sandy-grey beard in his worried way.

Kavanagh, in his gloomier moments, used to picture himself becoming like Captain Harrison. He was a harassed-looking little man, who was haunted by a nightmare-like dread of losing his ship and his ticket. He had a sickly wife and a brood of young children at home, and his indecision had prevented him from climbing any higher on the ladder of success than the rung which was represented by the command of the "Gairloch."

"Glass falling," mumbled the captain into his sparse beard, "sea rising ... in for a night of it...."

Kavanagh hardly heard him. His eyes glued to his glasses, he gazed with a passionate intensity at the abandoned vessel.

It was queer. He couldn't explain it—couldn't understand it! But there was something about that ship that made him feel that, at all costs, he *must* save her! He could no more turn tail and leave her to perish than if there had been human lives at stake. He could no more do it than a knight of old could calmly ride away and leave a distressed damsel making signals from a turret top. And, indeed, as her masts dipped and rose again in the sea, she did somehow seem to be making signals—personal signals—to him and to no one else: to be saying, "Come! You're surely not going to leave me to it, are you?"

"She'd be well worth salving," he said, trying to keep some of the eagerness out of his voice as he turned towards his captain. "Mean a lot of money ... if you could spare the hands——"

Captain Harrison shook his head. He looked almost terrified. But Kavanagh had seen the momentary gleam in his eyes at the mention of the money, and his hopes rose.

"I don't see how I'm going to spare the men," said the captain, "and besides what good would these chaps be for a job like that. I doubt if there's more than two or three of 'em have ever been in sail at all."

"She isn't a big ship, sir," urged Kavanagh. "If you could let me have half a dozen hands I could manage her all right."

Captain Harrison pulled a minute longer at his ragged beard; then broke out hurriedly, as if afraid that his own indecision might get the better of him again: "Well, have it your own way—your own responsibility, mind—and you'll have to ask for volunteers. I'm not going to order men away on a job like that. Madness, you know, really. I oughtn't to do it—oughtn't to do it——"

There was, as it turned out, no need to order. Out of the twenty-six hands comprising the deck department of the "Gairloch" a dozen volunteered at once, and Kavanagh had a hard job to pick his salvage crew.

Truth to tell, there wasn't much to pick among them! Only two had had a brief experience in sail. As for the rest, what they lacked in knowledge they made up in enthusiasm. The donkeyman unexpectedly manifested a romantic yearning to "'ave a trip in one o' them there," but him Captain Harrison, resolute for once, flatly declined to spare.

Kavanagh was hard put to it to hide a rueful grin when he saw his crowd ranged up before him. They were a scratch lot if ever there was one! He foresaw that it would be up to him to combine as best he could the duties of mate, second mate, bos'n, and general bottle-washer with those of temporary skipper of "'Maria'—Genoa."

Scratch lot or not, however, the salvage crew were mightily pleased with themselves as they pulled away for the barque, and they raised a highly creditable cheer by way of farewell to their shipmates lined up along the bulwarks of the "Gairloch."

One of the last things Kavanagh saw was Ferguson's hairy countenance thrust over the rail.

"Every yin to his taste!" bawled the engineer. "Ah wouldna trust ma precious life to thon bluidy auld windbag in the gale o' wund that's gaun to blaw the nicht!"

His last words were caught up and whirled away on one of the short, fierce gusts which blew out of the west at ever shorter intervals, and Kavanagh heard no more.

A scene of chaos welcomed him as he climbed aboard the "Maria." She had a big deck-load of lumber, which had broken adrift, and lay piled up against the temporary topgallant rail, together with an empty hencoop, a stove-in barrel, and a number of other miscellaneous items. That in itself was enough to account for the list of the vessel. Aloft she was in better case than a casual glance suggested. Her spars were all intact, in spite of the bad dusting she had evidently been through, but every sail had been blown out of the bolt-ropes, with the exception of the fore-lower topsail, and that was split from head to foot. The gale had evidently struck her when she was carrying a fair amount of canvas, and Kavanagh conjectured that the crew had turned panicky and made no attempt to save the ship, but had jumped at the chance of being taken off by some passing vessel.

He signalled to the "Gairloch," which was still standing by, that he was able to carry on, and with a farewell hoot of her siren she rolled off again on her homeward road. Soon her smoke was lost to view in the gathering dusk. The derelict was on her own now, for good or ill.

Kavanagh set his crew to work at once heaving the deck-load over the side, and himself went below, accompanied by one of his few "sail" men, a young seaman named Rawlings, to investigate matters below.

The sense of desolation which always pervades any place inhabited by man when man's presence is removed was strong upon him as soon as he began to descend the companion which led to the saloon. That he had looked for, however, and silence he had also looked for: so that it was with an unpleasant sensation of shock that he became suddenly aware of a strange voice speaking in rapid and monotonous tones, and in some language, too, which he could not at all make out.

There was someone on board all the time, then! And yet—it was a peculiar sort of voice—a voice with a strange, a hardly human ring in it—unnatural, uncanny. Kavanagh stopped short half-way down the companion. His scalp crept; indeed, he felt convinced that his cap must be standing at least a quarter of an inch off his head. He restrained, not without difficulty, a primitive impulse to bolt up on deck again—an impulse which the consciousness of Rawlings' round eyes and open mouth just behind him helped him to check.

The voice ceased as suddenly as it had begun, and the silence which followed it was worse than the sound.

"Wot the 'ell is it?" came the hoarse voice of Rawlings.

"Sounds like someone crazy," pronounced Kavanagh; "sick, perhaps, and they couldn't get him away——"

He pulled himself together with an effort, and they completed the descent into the saloon.

They stood together, Rawlings and he, in the little saloon, panelled with bird's-eye maple in the style once considered the last word in elegant ship decoration, with its shabby padded settees, its mahogany table marked with the rings of many glasses, its spotted and tarnished mirrors, and its teak medicine chest in the corner.

It was a sorrowful, haunted little place. A smell of stale cigar-smoke hung about it. The air was chilly, yet stuffy. The uncanny silence of the deserted ship was all around—a silence only intensified by the monotonous booming and crashing of the seas, and the occasionally spasmodic thrashing of a loose block on the deck overhead.

The mysterious voice broke forth anew in a torrent of unintelligible speech. The sound came this time almost as a relief to the tension. It was so unmistakably real, now that it was at closer quarters, that half its terrors fled.

"Whatever it is," exclaimed Kavanagh, "it's in here!"

Flinging open a door on his right hand, he stepped boldly in.

The next moment he burst into a shout of laughter. It was a large and imposing stateroom with a big teak bed—evidently the captain's, a relic of the days when the captain of a crack sailing ship was decidedly a somebody, and when, moreover, he frequently took his wife to sea with him. And in the middle of the bed was a brass cage containing the owner of the voice—a fine sulphur-crested cockatoo, which was even now pouring forth a flood of the choicest polyglot oaths Kavanagh had ever heard.

It was astonishing what a reaction that bird brought about. All the haunted air of the ship seemed to have been effectually dispelled. Kavanagh's spirits began to rise unreasonably as he continued his tour of his new command.

The sail locker yielded up only the remains of a fine-weather suit, mostly patches. Kavanagh whistled softly to himself as he fingered the thin canvas, and thought about the swiftly falling glass and the fierce gusts which blew ever more frequently out of the angry winter sunset.

Still, there was nothing for it but to make the best of a bad job, so, leaving one of his best men at the wheel, he set about the task of getting off the rags of the fore-lower topsail and bending the new (or rather the whole) sail in its place.

And what a job that was! Never to the day of his death will Kavanagh forget it. He had worked with scratch crews in his time, but never before with a crowd like those well-meaning steamer deck-hands who had never seen a sail in their lives at such close quarters.

Swearing, struggling, hanging on with teeth and nails, they sweated and toiled on their unaccustomed perch, until at last—it seemed like a miracle— all was as snug aloft as was possible in the circumstances. The chaos on deck was reduced to something approaching order, though the ship still lay over to it rather more than Kavanagh liked. And now, the watch being set and look-outs posted, he had time to do what he had been longing to do—find out, if he could, what the old ship's past had been.

He felt convinced that she was the product of some crack Aberdeen or Clydeside builder, for, in spite of her dirty and neglected condition, there was about her the unmistakable air of decayed gentility. The brass on capstan and wheel was so caked with rust and paint that the letters of the builder's name could not be discerned, and it was only by chance, while making an inspection of the miscellaneous junk in the lazarette, that he made the great discovery.

This was, in the first place, nothing more important than an old ship's bell with a crescent-shaped fragment broken out. It had evidently been thrown down there when it was replaced by a new one. It was thick with dirt and verdigris; but, pressed for time as he was, an instinct of curiosity made him linger while he scraped off some of the deposit with his knife to see if anything lay beneath.

His first find was a date—1869.

"Hallo! This gets interesting!" he exclaimed. "Here's a letter—'D'—no, 'P,' 'L' something, an 'M,' another 'M'——"

His breath began to come fast with excitement. He scraped away harder than ever.

"It *can't* be," he gasped, sitting back on his heels, "but, by George, it *is*!... The 'Plinlimmon'!"

Possibly few people outside that comparatively restricted circle which is closely interested in sailing ships and their records could understand the feeling of almost reverential awe with which the mate of the "Gairloch" gazed at the dim lettering on that old broken bell. To most laymen—indeed, to many seamen of the more modern school—it would have stood for nothing but an old outworn ship—a good ship, no doubt, in her day, a day long since over and done.

But to Kavanagh and to his like the name "Plinlimmon" had a very different significance.

Some ships there are whose names remain as names to conjure with long after they themselves are gone—names about which yarns will be spun and songs sung while still any live who have felt their spell. Such a ship was the "James Baines" of mighty memory; such also were the glorious "Thermopylæ," the lovely "Mermerus"; such the evergreen "Cutty Sark" and her forerunner "The Tweed." And—though perhaps in a lesser degree—such was also the "Plinlimmon."

And to Kavanagh she was even more.

She was like something belonging peculiarly to his own youth. She was inextricably interwoven with the memories of his boyhood, of his first voyage—those memories which for him now held the wistful golden glamour of youth departed.

For, though he had never before this moment beheld her with his bodily eyes, he had been brought up, as it were, in the "Plinlimmon" tradition. There had been an old fellow in his first ship—they called him Old Paul. He had served in the "Plinlimmon" in the days when she was commanded by the famous "Bully" Rogers: had, indeed, enjoyed the signal honour of being kicked off the poop by that nautical demigod. He was a hoary old ruffian, was Old Paul, but a seaman of the old stamp; and he had that curious, almost poetic, delight in the beauty of a ship which belonged to so many unlettered old seadogs in the days of sail.

Kavanagh had sat and listened to that old man's yarns for many and many an hour. The name "Plinlimmon" recalled to him a hundred memories he had thought forgotten. He almost seemed to hear the ghostly echo of the gruff old voice: "Ah, them was ships, them was, sonny.... When Bully Rogers set a sail, w'y, 'e *set* it.... Number One canvas, 'is royals was, an' they 'ad to stop there till it blew outer the bolt-ropes.... 'Hell or Melbourne' ... that was the game in them days in the ol' 'Plinlimmon.'..."

Why, he had all but forgotten Old Paul.... Where was the old chap now, he wondered.... Dead, no doubt, long ago.... He must have been seventy and more then, though he never owned to more than fifty-two....

But in the meantime there were other things to think of. The ship to bring into port ... the glass falling ... the wind and sea rising.... He turned away from the old bell and its memories and went back on deck.

The light was all but gone, and before the strength of the westerly wind the old ship was foaming gallantly along under her scanty sail, leaving a seething white wake faintly luminous in the dusk—the wind all the while in her rigging humming the song of the storm.

Just for a moment Kavanagh's heart sank at the thought of that fine weather lower topsail. Oh, for a bolt or two of Bully Rogers' Number One canvas, he thought; but it was only for a moment.

A curious exaltation gripped him.... "By God, she *shall* do it!" he said to the sea and the darkness.

Looking back in after years upon the events of the next few days, Kavanagh could never feel quite certain how long they really occupied.

Time—there *was* no time! There was just a never-ending succession of low, hurrying, ragged-edged clouds chasing over a confusion of white-crested waves that came charging perpetually out of the dim vapour that shrouded the meeting of sea and sky. There must have been days—there must have been nights. But he hardly noticed either their coming or their going. He was intent, his whole being was intent, on one thing, and one thing only—saving that old ship from her old rival the sea.

How they worked, those amazing, those indomitable steamboat-men! It was as if the spirits of all the "Plinlimmon's" old sailors had come back to join in the struggle. They fought with strange monsters in the shape of sails and ropes, they groped in tangles and labyrinths of unaccustomed rigging; and their great hearts kept them going. While there was breath in their bodies to work they pumped, and when they could do no more they dropped in their tracks and slept the sleep of sheer exhaustion.

Once the whole crew was washed overboard clinging to the lee forebrace, only to be sucked back again with the next roll of the ship. Once Kavanagh heard a man pouring out a flood of the vilest oaths in a tone of mild expostulation, as he nursed a hand streaming with blood which had been jammed between a block and the pin-rail. And once he remembered seeing that lower topsail, bent with such pains and peril, simply fade out of the bolt-ropes and be seen no more. It didn't split or tear. It just vanished....

But there always seemed to him to be a sort of dream-like atmosphere about the whole thing. He was never quite sure what did happen and what didn't happen. It was impossible on the face of it, for instance, that Old Paul should have been there hauling with the rest—yet at the time Kavanagh was quite sure that he saw him. It was also impossible that there should have been a dozen men on the yard when there were only half a dozen in the whole blessed ship—yet Kavanagh was equally sure at the time that he saw and counted them. He even remembered some of their faces—a huge fellow with a bare, tattooed chest, in particular, that he hadn't seen about the ship before.... Not that he ever mentioned it to anyone else. He might have been asleep and dreamed it, for all he knew. Still, it served a useful purpose at the time. It put heart into him. And he needed it before the end!...

At last—at long last—came a grey dawn that broke through ragged clouds upon a sea heaving as with spent passion, upon a handful of weary, indomitable men, upon an old ship that still lived!

Kavanagh was suddenly aware that he was tired—dog-tired; that his wrists were red-raw with the chafing of his oilskins; that the weight of uncounted days and nights without sleep was weighing down his eyelids like lead.

But he had won—he had won! And he had commanded the "Plinlimmon"! Whatever the years to come might bring or take away, they could never rob him of that glory. They could bring him no greater prize.

There was a yell from the look-out, and a faint answering shout came back out of the grey dawn.

"The ba-arque, aho-oy!"

A boat scraped against the ship's side. One by one, a succession of familiar faces topped the "Plinlimmon's" rail. The "Gairloch's" donkeyman, the "Gairloch's" cook, the "Gairloch's" boy clutching and being desperately clutched by the "Gairloch's" cat!

Last of all, Ferguson climbed heavily over the rail and sat down on a spare spar, wiping his face with a lump of waste.

"A steamer—a Dago—rin the auld girl doon," he said, "an' the swine sheered off an' left us to droon, for all he knew."

He paused a moment, then went on, his voice rising suddenly to a lament:

"She wasna muckle to look at ... but, man, she'd gran' guts in her!"

Kavanagh let him have the last word. In the circumstances, he felt he could afford it.

ORANGES

THE clipper ship "Parisina" lay becalmed off the Western Islands. The gallant Nor'-East Trade which had hummed steadily through her royals for ten blue and golden days and star-sown nights had tailed away ignominiously into a succession of fitful, faint, and baffling airs which kept the wearied crew constantly hauling the yards at the bidding of every shift of the variable breeze, and withal scarcely served to give the clipper leeway; and had died off last of all into a flat calm.

She lay there as still as if she were at anchor. Her sails drooped against the masts with no more movement than banners slowly dropping to silent dust in the nave of some great cathedral. Their shadows on the white deck were clearly defined as shapes cut out of black paper. There was no sound aloft, not so much as the churring of a rope stirring in its sheave: only a faint creak by whiles, as the ship lifted imperceptibly on the long, low swing of the ocean.

A light haze hung over the outlines of the islands and over the horizon beyond, so that it was impossible to define where sea ended and sky began. A couple of fruit schooners about half a mile distant hovered above their own motionless reflections, like butterflies poised above flowers. So complete was the calm that even they could not catch a breath sufficient to keep them moving. They looked almost as if they were suspended in some new element, neither water nor air, yet partaking of the character of both.

Old "Sails" sat on the forehatch, spectacles on nose, stitching busily away at the bolt-rope of a royal which had come out second best from an argument with the stormy westerlies. A tall, thin, old man, he looked as he sat there with his shanks folded under him like one of those long-legged crabs the Cornish folk call "Gramfer Jenkins." He had a short, white beard stained with chewing tobacco, and as he worked his jaws moved rhythmically in time with the movements of his active needle.

A boat had pulled out from the nearest island with baskets of fruit, and its owner, a swarthy negroid Portuguese with a bright handkerchief bound pirate-wise about his frizzy hair, was driving bargains with the men of the watch below amid much rough banter and chaff. The men laughed, called, shouted to one another, threw the fruit from hand to hand, eager as children.

From the main deck came the steady slish-scrape of holystones; the mate had taken advantage of the opportunity the calm offered of bringing the "Parisina's" already bone-white planking nearer to that unattainable perfection of immaculate cleanliness which only exists in the dreams of New England housewives and particular-minded mates of sailing vessels. Mr. Billing, the mate, was an insignificant little man with sandy hair and a peculiar habit of sniffing to himself like a beetle-hunting hedgehog. He sniffed now as he hovered with a perpetual fussy watchfulness among the humped figures of his watch, squatting over their task like worshipping bronzes. Mr. Billing was of the housewifely type of mate. A man secretly of little courage and no initiative, he disliked the "Parisina's" paces intensely. He was nervous of ships as some lifelong horsemen are nervous of horses. Calms, on the other hand, with the consequent time they afforded for ritual scouring and painting of wood and metal, he delighted in much as a house-proud woman of the suburbs delights in spring cleaning.

The men growled among themselves, sailor fashion, as they worked. "Gimme ol' Stiff afore this 'ere bloody scrubbin'," said one. "Same 'ere," said another. "Why can't it blow up ag'in, I says? A year an' a 'arf's bloomin' pay I've got comin' to me at Green's 'Ome, an' if it wasn't for this 'ere blessed calm I'd be six 'undred mile nearer spendin' of it by now." "Sailorizin's all right," grumbled a third. "It's this 'ere darned 'ouse-maidin' as gets my goat."

Up in the "Parisina's" tiny chart-room Captain Fareweather—he was known through all the ports of the Southern Hemisphere, for good and sufficient reasons, as "Old Foul-weather"—carefully wetted his finger, and with a furrowed brow turned a leaf and prepared to make a fresh entry in the "Parisina's" log-book.

Old Foul-weather was not fond of his pen, a fact to which the crabbed and painful handwriting which filled the preceding pages bore eloquent testimony. Spelling was an anguish to him; and indeed it is doubtful whether the hours of endurance and anxiety which the entries in the book represented were one half as irksome to him as the labour of recording them. But there were on this occasion other reasons for his look of depression.

Captain Fareweather detested calms as much as his mate liked them. It might be said of him that he had one absorbing passion in his life. He lived that the "Parisina" might make good passages; especially, perhaps, that she might beat her rival, the "Alcazar." If she did, life was worth living, if she didn't, it was not. Certainly it was not for those unfortunate beings who happened to be his shipmates for the time being.

"'Tain't good reading," said Old Foul-weather to himself, as he carefully blotted the new entry—it consisted of one word, "Same"—and replaced ink and pen.

He traced the lines of the uncongenial record with a stumpy forefinger.

"'Winds puffey and varible. Ship scarcely moveing.'

"'Very light airs.'

"'Dead calm.'

"Wonder where old Jones and his blooming 'Alcazar' are," he reflected. He sighed and closed the book.

No faintest air entered the stuffy little room. The voices of the men as they growled and grumbled over their work came clearly to him through the open port. From below there drifted up a pleasant tinkle and chink of crockery and cutlery as the steward laid the cabin dinner.

Through the open companion he could see the helmsman lolling beside the wheel, his outstretched arm resting along its rim, his fingers loosely gripping the spokes. He had for once the easiest job in the ship. It was not always so, for, though the "Parisina," rightly handled, steered like a lamb, she needed humouring as much as a horse with a fine mouth. He was a handsome fellow, swarthy and black-eyed; under the thick growth of hair on his broad chest showed faintly some tattooed device in red and blue, a relic of his younger and less hirsute years.

A barefooted apprentice padded up the poop ladder and struck one bell: a mellow note that hung trembling on the still air, till it quivered away into silence high up among the sleeping royals. The boy wore a patched shirt and ragged dungaree trousers, and his arms and legs were burned black as mahogany by the tropic sun. He was a tall lad, with the lanky grace of adolescence; a faint down was just showing on his upper lip, and the sun gleaming upon the growth of fair hair on his arms and chest made him look as if powdered with gold dust.

Captain Fareweather sighed, put the log-book by, and descended to the cabin. McAllister, the second mate, a big-boned Aberdonian, perennially hungry, was already there, with one eye on the hash the steward had just set before the Old Man's chair. He composed his features into an appropriate cast of pious decorum as the captain took his seat and placed his hand before his eyes for his customary grace. This rite was silent and lengthy; but Captain Fareweather's officers knew better than to betray impatience or inattention while it lasted. Legend said that a second mate, greatly daring, had once begun to nibble his bread before the captain had finished, and at once there had come a voice from the behind the hand, like the voice of Mitche Manitou the Mighty, "Ye irreverential devil, can't ye see I'm sayin' grace?"

It was an uncomfortable meal. The skipper was moody, and McAllister was horribly nervous in consequence. The few small pebbles of conversation he cast into the silence fell with an appalling splash which instantly covered him with scarlet confusion to the tips of his large red ears, and it was with profound thankfulness that he welcomed the appearance of the mate with a basket of oranges.

"I thought you'd like a few," explained Mr. Billing, "for dinner. They're good. A bumboat feller brought 'em alongside."

"Bluid oranges," exclaimed McAllister. He dug his strong square teeth into the glistening rind, and the red juice squirted over his bony knuckles. "They've ay the best flavour."

They seemed to light up the cabin like golden lamps, warm, glowing, still with the sunlight glory about them. Their fragrance filled the place, aromatic, pungent, cloying.

"I don't care for 'em," said the Captain suddenly. "The smell of 'em— too strong."

He pushed back his chair as he spoke.

"Stuffy," he muttered; "glad when we can get way on her again."

He stumped off up the companion ladder: a square, stocky figure of a man, short-necked, broad of shoulder. The two mates looked at each other significantly.

"What bug's bit the auld deevil now?" said McAllister in a conspiratorial whisper.

"God knows!" returned Mr. Billing. "He's always this way when he can't be at his cracking on. Old madman!"

"He's a fine seaman, though," replied McAllister. "I'll say that for him."

"Fine seaman!" breathed Mr. Billing bitterly. "You wait till he shakes the sticks out of her one fine night. That's all."

Old Foul-weather stood leaning on the poop railing, looking out across the still expanse of the waters with eyes which did not see the haze-dimmed islands or the motionless schooners poised above their reflected selves. Strange—something had stirred in its sleep a little while since at the sight of those very schooners—something had turned in its sleep and sighed at the sight of the young apprentice in his sunburned youth. And just now, with the scent of the oranges, it had stirred, turned again, sighed again, awakened—the memory of Conchita!

Conchita—why, he hadn't thought of her for years. He wouldn't like to say how many years. He had had plenty of other things to occupy his mind. Work, for one thing. And ships. Plenty of other women had come into his life and gone out of it, too, since then. Queer, how things came back to you; so that they seemed all of a sudden to have happened no longer ago than yesterday....

He was in just such a schooner as one of those yonder at the time. The "John and Jane" her name was—a pretty little thing, sailed like a witch, too. Lost, he had heard, a year or two ago on a voyage over to Newfoundland with a cargo of salt. It had been his first voyage South. He had been in nothing but billyboys and Geordie brigs until then. He had run his last ship in London. The skipper was a hard-mouthed old ruffian, the mate a trifle worse. Between them the boy Jim had a tough time of it. Then one day the captain caught him in the act of purloining the leg of a duck destined for his own dinner; and, pursuing him with a short length of rope with the amiable intention of flaying hell out of him, fell head foremost on the top of his own ballast and lay for dead. He wasn't dead: far from it. But young Jim thought he was. So he pulled himself ashore in the dinghy and set off along Wapping High Street with only the vaguest idea where he was going.

He stuck to the water-side as a hunted fox sticks to cover. The Tower he passed quickly by: it looked too much like a lock-up, he thought. Presently he came to a church, and a big clock sticking out over the roadway; and close by a wharf where schooners were loading, and among them the "John and Jane."

He liked the looks of her. She was clean and fresh and sweet-smelling. And the mate, who was superintending the lowering of some cases into the hold, had a red, jolly face that took his fancy.

The boy Jim peered down into the hold. It was full almost to the hatch-coamings. She must be going to sail soon.

The red-faced mate had given his last order, and was coming down the gangway with the virtuous and anticipatory look of one at ease with his own conscience after a spell of arduous toil, and about to reward himself for the same with liquid refreshment.

Young Fareweather stepped forward, his heart thumping.

"Was you wanting a hand, mister?"

The red-faced man looked at him consideringly.

"A hand? A s'rimp, you mean!" He guffawed slapping his hands on his fat thighs, a man well pleased with his own joke.

"Ah con do a mon's work, though," the youngster insisted.

"Ye can, can ye? Can ye steer."

"Aye, Ah con that."

"Can ye reef an' furl, splice a rope-yarn, peel potatoes and cook the cabin dinner of a Sunday?"

"Ah con that."

The mate roared.

"Sort of a admirayble bright 'un, I can see," he said. "Well, I tell you what. Here's the skipper comin' down the wharf. We'll see what he says."

The captain, a fierce-looking little man with bushy eyebrows, indulged in a smile at the recital of Jim's reputed accomplishments.

"Take him if ye like," he said, "and, listen, you, boy" (bending the bushy brows on Jim), "if you're tellin' lies, it's the rope's-end you'll taste, my lad."

He spent the night curled up on a box in the corner of the galley, listening with one ear to the yarns of the old one-eyed shipkeeper, the other cocked for the ominous tread of the dreaded policeman. But dawn came, and brought no policeman, and by noon the "John and Jane" was dropping downstream with the tide.

It seemed to the boy Jim like a foretaste of Heaven. The captain was a kindly man for all his appearance of ferocity, the mate easier still. No one got kicked; nobody went without his grub—incidentally he was relieved to find that nothing further was said about cooking the cabin dinner; wonder of wonders, nobody was so much as sworn at seriously. True, the amiable mate was the most foul-mouthed man he had ever come across before or since. But then, hard words break no bones, especially on board ship, and the mate's repertoire was generally looked on as something in the nature of a polite accomplishment: something like conjuring tricks or making pictures out of ink blots.

It was all a wonder to him, just as Oporto, whither the "John and Jane" was bound, was a wonder to him after the cold stormy North Sea, the bleak streets of Newcastle and Wapping which so far had been his only idea of seaports. The schooner, as has already been said, was an easy ship, and in port the hands had plenty of time to themselves. He liked the sun, the light, the warmth, the colour. He liked the laughing, lazy, careless children of the

South. He liked the many-coloured houses that climbed the steep streets
of the old town—and the bathing in the great river—and the little stuffy
wineshops with their mixed smell of sour wine and sawdust and stale cigar-
smoke and onions—and the bells that chimed day long, night long, from
hidden convents in green gardens behind high walls. And the oranges——

The day he first saw Conchita, he had gone off for a walk by himself,
and, the day being hot, had lain down by the roadside to rest. And as he
lay there half asleep, lulled by the shrill song of the cicalas in the grass all
round him, plop! something bounced on to his chest, rolled a little way, and
lay still.

He reached out his hand and picked it up. An orange! Its skin was still
warm with the sun, and it had that indefinable bloom on it that belongs to
all fruit newly gathered. And then he looked round to see where it had come
from, and saw—Conchita!

Conchita with her dark, vivacious little face, her eyes black as sloes, her
red lips open in a wide laugh that showed a row of perfect teeth—Conchita
with her full white sleeves under her stiff embroidery jacket, her wide gay-
coloured petticoats, her dainty white-stockinged ankles and little slippered
feet; why, she was almost like a talking doll, Jim thought, that he had seen
in a big toyshop in Newcastle, and wished he had the money to buy for his
sister! He felt as awkward, as clumsy with her as a boy with a doll. Goodness
knows how they understood one another, those two young things! There is
a sort of freemasonry, somehow or other, among young things that laughs
at such difficulties as language. She knew a little broken English, which she
was immensely proud of. She had picked it up at school from an English
playmate. But Jim knew nothing but his own East Coast brand of his native
speech. However, understand one another they did, somehow or other. He
learnt her name, of course, and how she laughed at his attempts to say it
as she said it! He learned, also, that she was sixteen, and that she was to be
married some day to old João the muleteer, but that she did not like him
because of "ees faze—o-ah, long, lak' dees!" And she stretched out her arms
to their full extent to indicate it. But she "lak' Ing-lees sailor, o-ah ver-ree,
ver-ree much"—and she "giv' you—o-ah, ever so many orange—lak' dees!"
And she made a wide circle with her arms to show their number.

The boy went back to his ship in a kind of dream. Her warm Southern
nature was riper far than his. He was swept clean off his feet by the fervour
of her unashamed yet innocent lovemaking—by the feel of her warm body,
of her warm lips, of her rounded cheeks soft and glowing, as sun-warmed
oranges. Of course he went again—and many times again—and then there
came the last night before the "John and Jane" was to sail.

It had been arranged that for once he was not to go alone. Perhaps Conchita, strange little blend of impulse and sophistication, had judged it best that their leave-taking should not be an *affaire à deux*. Jim was to bring some of his shipmates along: and Conchita would bring also some of the other girls. And it would "be fon—o-ah, yees, soch fon!"

He remembered the queer feeling of shrinking that came over him as they set out on that fatal expedition. What had happened he never really knew. Perhaps one of his shipmates had blabbed about it in the little wineshop on the quay; perhaps one of the other girls. What mattered was that somehow the jealous João, with the "faze long, lak' dees," had heard of it!

They went stumbling and whispering up the lane that led out of the town. He could remember the warm scent of that autumn night and the way the wind went sighing through the broad, dark leaves of the orange groves and the gnarled cork trees that bordered the stony mule-track by which they climbed. They passed a little inn by the wayside, where a man was playing a guitar and singing an interminable ballad full of wailing, sobbing notes, in the melancholy minor key common to folk-melodies the world over.

The moon was shining through the trees when they came to the rendezvous. They had brought sacks with them, and the girls shook the fragrant globes down while they gathered them into heaps.

And then, suddenly, all was changed. It was like a nightmare. There were lights, and people shouting. The girls screamed. Conchita cried out, "Run, run!" She clung round his neck, fondling his face, weeping. There was a fierce face, a lifted hand, something that sang as it fled. And Conchita was all of a sudden limp in his arms, her face, with a look of hurt surprise in its wide eyes and fallen mouth, drooping backward like a flower broken on its stalk. She seemed to be sinking, sinking away from him, like a drowned thing sinking into deep water....

He did not know who dragged that limp thing from his numb arms. He did not know who hustled him away, shouting in his ear, "Run, ye damned fool, run! Them bloody Dagoes'll knife the lot of us." He remembered being hurried down the lane, and past the lighted inn where the man was still at his interminable wailing songs. And then—no more, until he came to himself under the smelly oil lamp in the familiar forecastle.

The "John and Jane" sailed at dawn....

Captain Fareweather sighed, shifted his elbows on the rail, stiffened himself suddenly, and stood erect. The look of the sea had changed. Its surface was blurred as if a hand had been drawn gently across it.

One after the other the two schooners began to steal slowly, very slowly across his line of vision. He cast an eye aloft. There was a slight tremor in the hitherto motionless clew of the main royal.

He sniffed the coming wind as a dog sniffs the scent of its accustomed quarry; then he walked briskly across to the break of the poop and, leaning his hands on the rail, called to the mate.

"Mister!"

"Sir?"

"Stand by to square away your main yard! I think we'll get a breeze afore two bells."

He walked the poop fore and aft, rubbing his hands and whistling a little tune.

There was a scamper of bare feet on the planking. Men sang out as they hauled on the braces, "Yo-heu-yoi-hee!" Blocks sang shrill as fifes, reef points beat a tattoo on the tautened canvas. The sails filled with loud clappings. Out of the north-east came the wind — shattering the calm mirror of the sea into a million splinters — filling the royals like the cheeks of the trumpeting angels of the Judgment — burying under its mounded confusion the very memory of the vanished calm, even as the years lay mounded over the dead face of Conchita, whom the gods loved too well.....

"We'll beat that bloody 'Alcazar' yet, mister," said Captain Fareweather.

SEATTLE SAM SIGNS ON

"IT'S what I'm always tellin' you, Mike," said Captain Bascomb severely, "you're too rough with 'em."

Mr. Michael Doyle, mate of the skysail yarder "Bride of Abydos," was usually nearly as handy with his tongue as he was with his fists, which was saying a good deal. But on this occasion he was, for once in his life, fairly stumped. He opened and shut his mouth several times like a landed fish, but, like a fish, remained speechless.

"Too rough with 'em, that's what you are," pursued the skipper. "You should use a bit o' tact. You shouldn't keep kickin' 'em. I'm a humane man myself, and I tell you I take it very hard—very hard indeed I do—to have my ship avoided as if we'd got plague on board just because I've got a rip-roarin' great gazebo of a mate from the County Cork that doesn't know when to keep his feet to himself. When I was a nipper they learned me to count ten before I kicked. That's what you want to do. Twenty for the matter o' that."

Captain Bascomb was a hard case, though anyone overhearing the foregoing remarks might have thought otherwise. He was also a tough nut. Men who spoke from personal experience said, and said with deep emotion, that he was both these things, as well as other things less fitted for polite mention: so presumably it was true.

Now, while there are undeniably times and seasons when it is a valuable asset for a shipmaster to have the character of a tough nut and a hard case, there are equally conceivable circumstances when such a reputation may be a decidedly inconvenient possession. And it was precisely such a set of circumstances which had arisen on the day in late autumn when the conversation just recorded took place.

The "Bride of Abydos" lay alongside the lumber mill wharf at Victoria. Her cargo of lumber was all on board. And she would have been ready to sail for home on the next morning's tide but for one trifling and inconvenient particular—namely, that she was without a crew.

This regrettable discrepancy was due to two principal reasons. In the first place, the rumour of a discovery of gold, or copper, or aluminium, or something of a metallic nature up in the Rocky Mountains had had the inevitable effect of inducing the ship's company of the "Bride of Abydos" to abandon as one man their nautical calling, and depart for the interior of British Columbia with an unbounded enthusiasm which would only be surpassed by the enthusiasm with which they would doubtless return to it in less than three months' time.

But it would be useless to deny that Captain Bascomb's fame as a tough nut—a fame to which the ungrudging tributes of his late crew had given a considerable local fillip—was the outstanding cause for the coyness manifested by eligible substitutes about coming forward to fill the vacant berths in the "Bride of Abydos's" forecastle.

Hence it was that gloom sat upon Captain Bascomb's brow, and a reflected gloom upon that of Mr. Michael Doyle—a gloom which was graphically expressed by the steward when he imparted to the black doctor in confidence the news that the Old Man was lookin' about as pleasant as a calf's daddy.

Mr. Doyle delicately brushed the crumbs from his waistcoat, and cleared his throat cautiously by way of preparing the ground for another conversational opening.

"What do you keep making that row for?" demanded the skipper. "You put me in mind of a cock chicken that's just learnin' to crow! If you do it again I'll mix you some cough stuff—and I'll see you swallow it too."

"I was only goin' to say——" began Mr. Doyle in aggrieved tones.

"Goin' to say, were you? Well, if you've got anything to say that'll show me how to make a crew that can work the 'Bride of Abydos' out of a nigger grub sp'iler and a hen-faced boob of an eavesdropping Cockney steward"—here he paused to relieve his feelings by adroitly launching a cuspidor at the inquiring countenance of Cockney George as it protruded from the pantry door—"you can say it," continued the skipper; "if not, you needn't! I'm in no mood for polite conversation, and that's a fact."

Silence and profound gloom descended once again upon the cabin and its occupants, while the fluttered and indignant George, still palpitating at the recollection of his narrow escape from the captain's unexpected projectile, slippered gingerly off to enjoy a growl with the black cook, who was sitting in his galley crooning the songs of Zion in a discreet undertone to the carefully muted strains of his concertina.

And just at that moment the gangway creaked loudly beneath a heavy tread, and a stranger stepped on board.

He was a large man with a large, flabby face, in which a large cigar was carelessly stuck as if to indicate the approximate position of the mouth: a loose-lipped mouth which looked, if possible, even more unpleasant when it smiled than when it scowled.

"Say, looks like someone's feelin' kinder peeved," observed the new-comer, pushing the skipper's late missile with his toe. "Cap'n aboard, stooard?"

"Ho, yus, he's on board right enough," responded George. "Frowed this 'ere at me 'ead just now, 'e did. Whatcher want?" he inquired suspiciously. "'Cos if it's tracks or anyfink o' that, I ain't goin' to let you in, not on your sweet life I ain't! Ever see a blinkin' gorilla wiv the toofache? 'Cos that's 'im—see! Just abart as safe to go near as wot 'e is—see! You take my tip and 'op it! Beat it for the tall timbers! Go while the goin's good!"

"That's right all right," responded the stranger cordially. "I guess I'll just walk right in and introdooce myself."

He stepped briskly along the alleyway and tapped on the cabin door.

A growl like that of a wounded jaguar was the only response, but, taking this as a permission to enter, the visitor projected his head, not without caution, round the edge of the door.

"G' mornin', Cap'n—g' mornin', mister," he said heartily. "Pardon me breezin' along this way, but I've a hunch you and me might be able to do business. I understand you're in a bit of a difficulty regardin' a crew."

Captain Bascomb regarded him for a few seconds without speaking. A remarkable variety of emotions might have been seen chasing one another across his countenance as he did so—surprise, incredulity, and joy chief among them.

"I am," he said slowly. "I am, and that's a fact, Mr.—— I didn't quite get your name."

"Grover—Samuel Grover—Seattle Sam to most folks around these parts," replied the stranger, making bold to enter and take a seat. "Fine ship you've got here, Cap'n!"

"Ship's all right," responded the skipper curtly.

He didn't seem able to take his eyes off Mr. Grover's face. It wasn't a beautiful face, either; to be quite candid, it verged upon the repulsive. But Captain Bascomb gazed at it as if it had been the face of his first love. Seattle Sam flattered himself he was making a good impression.

"See here, Cap'n," he went on, "I've a vurry nice bunch of b'ys up at my li'l' place on Cormorant Street. Prime sailormen every one of 'em. And I'd just love to ship 'em along with you. But" —he leaned forward and tapped his fat finger on the table—"here's the snag! Speakin' as man to man, Cap'n, you ain't asackly parpular."

"Oh, I'm not, ain't I?" said Captain Bascomb, bristling. "Well, if that's all you've come to say, the sooner you beat it out of here the better! As I was saying to my mate here only just now, I'm in no mood for polite conversation—not to say personal remarks of an offensive nature——"

"Not so fast, Cap'n, not so fast," said Seattle Sam hastily, taking the precaution to hook towards him the companion to the captain's earlier missile, ostensibly that he might put it to the purpose for which it was designed, but really in the interests of disarmament. "What I was just leadin' up to was this. I guess I can fix things for you good. But I guess I can't do it without a sort of a li'l' frameup."

At this point Mr. Doyle reluctantly withdrew, in obedience to a simple wireless message from his superior, and strain his ears as he might from his post at the head of the companion he could hear no more than a mumble of voices drifting up from below.

The conference was a lengthy one, so much so that Mr. Doyle had long grown tired of waiting when the tinkle of glasses indicated that it was drawing to a close.

"Well, here's towards ye, Cap'n," came the slightly raised voice of Seattle Sam, "an' to our li'l' trip together!"

The captain's guest had hardly got out of the alleyway before Mr. Doyle came clattering down the companion with his eyes bulging.

"Is that big stiff goin' to sign on wid us?" he inquired in a reverential whisper, his native Munster more honeyed than ever, as always in moments of deep emotion.

"He is, Mike," returned the skipper, in accents broken by feeling.

"Can I have him in my watch?" asked Mr. Doyle.

"Mike, you can."

"And can I—can I kick him whenever I like?" pursued the mate in the supplicating tones of a reciter giving an impersonation of a little child asking Santa Claus for a toy drum.

But at this point Captain Bascomb's feelings overcame him altogether, and, leaping from his seat, he seized his astonished second in command firmly yet gracefully round the middle, and proceeded to give a highly spirited rendering of the Tango Argentina as performed in that country.

George, who was observing matters from his usual point of vantage, flew to describe the portent to his crony in the galley.

"Dat's a bery dangerous man," said the doctor, "a bery biolent, uncontrollabous kin' of a man, sonny! Ah jus' done drop mah ol' pipe in de cabin soup one mawnin', an' Ah tell you Ah wuz skeered for mah life. An' Ah tell you what, bo'—Ah'se skeered o' dat man when he's lookin' ugly, but Ah'se ten times, twenty times, hundred times skeereder when he's lookin' pleased.... An' when he gits dancin'— —" And he rolled his woolly head till it nearly fell off his shoulders.

Meanwhile Mr. Samuel Grover was stepping out briskly in the direction of his boarding-house for seamen in the pleasant thoroughfare known as Cormorant Street. The name was a singularly appropriate one, for Mr. Grover and his like had long gorged there upon sailormen. He hummed pleasantly to himself as he walked, and the rapidity with which he twirled his cigar round his large loose mouth indicated to those who knew the man that he was feeling on unusually good terms with himself and the world.

"Now, b'ys," he cried, rubbing his fat hands together as he surveyed the dozen or so of depressed-looking sailormen who were playing draw poker for Chinese stinkers in the bar of his modest establishment, "now, b'ys, I've gotten a real fine ship for the lot o' ye."

The old habitués of his place looked at one another with dawning suspicion. They had encountered this air of extravagant geniality before.

"W-w-wot's name-of-er?" inquired Billy Stutters, so called by reason of a slight impediment in his speech. It never took him less than a minute to get up steam, but as soon as he was under way the words came with a rush, like water from a stopped-up drain whence the obstruction has been suddenly removed.

"The 'Bride of Abbeydoes,'" said Mr. Grover, "and a damn fine ship too."

You could have heard a pin drop for a minute or two while his audience digested this news. Ginger Jack, who was an old man-of-war's man, and as hard a case as any of the King's bad bargains who ever drifted under the Red Duster, was heard to observe that he warn't goin' to sign in no blinkin' "Abbeydoes," nor "Abbeydon't" neither for the matter o' that. Billy Stutters, after a mighty effort, was understood to second the amendment.

"Ho, you ain't, ain't you?" said Mr. Grover with scathing irony. "An' wot makes your Royal 'Ighnesses that bloomin' partic'lar, may I ask?"

"B-b-b-becos-I've-bin-in-'er-afore," said Billy, sulkily, "an' the sk-k-kipper-kicked-me!"

"Did he so?" commented Mr. Grover facetiously. "I thought maybe you was goin' to say he kissed you.... Now, look 'ere, b'ys," he continued, assuming all the powers of persuasion he could muster; "I guess you've gotten cold feet about the 'Bride of Abbeydoes.' You take it from me, she ain't so black as what she's painted. Not by a jugful. I don't mind admittin', man to man, Captain Bascomb's a hard case. And Mister Doyle, well, I reckon he's another. But they're all right with a crowd of smart, handy boys like yourselves. You ain't a bunch o' greasers or sodbusters from way back that don't know a deadeye from a fourfold purchase. You're the sort o' crowd as a skipper won't find no fault with, as he'll be proud to see about his ship. And just to show I'm in earnest, I'm goin' to sign on in the 'Bride of Abbeydoes' myself. Fair an' square. I'm about doo to run across and see the home-folks in London, England. I've a fancy to take a turn at sailorizin' again. An' I like a fast ship. Now then, b'ys, is it a go? That's the style. The drinks are on the house!"

"Nice sort o' state of affairs," observed Mr. Grover a little later to his factotum in the privacy of the den he called his office. "A lot of ungrateful swabs I've been keepin'—keepin', mind you—for best part of two weeks, and they ups with their 'Won't sign 'ere' 'n' 'Ain't goin' to sail there' as if they was bloomin' lords. Well, well! I'll learn 'em. Don't I hope Mr. Bucko Doyle'll put it across 'em good and hard, that's all!

"Why, in the old days in 'Frisco," he continued dreamily, "you could ship a corp and no questions asked. And as for sailormen—well, you didn't consult 'em. And quite right too. A lot they know about what's good for 'em—a bunch of idle, extravagant swine! Warn't it all for their good to get 'em shipped off to sea sharp afore they'd got time to get into trouble and go fillin' up the jail, I ask you? And then you get a lot of meddlin' psalm-singin' idjits as don't know the first thing about the class o' men people like me 'ave got to deal with. Psha!"

And Mr. Grover set about filling a sea-chest with an assortment of old newspapers and empty bottles which would have struck his future shipmates, had they been there to see, as a curious outfit for a Cape Horn passage.

The next day bright and early he attended with his crowd at the shipping office, where, having duly heard the ship's articles mumbled over, the party appended their signatures and marks thereto and became duly members of the crew of the "Bride of Abydos." The morning was fine and sunny, and every one was in high good-humour. Captain Bascomb's face was wreathed in smiles, and the wink to which Seattle Sam treated him when no one was looking elicited an even huger one in reply.

All the same, a joke is a joke, and Mr. Grover considered that it was carrying the joke a bit too far when the third mate, a big apprentice just out of his time, ordered him to tail on to the topsail halyards or he'd wonder what hit him. However, he complied with the order with as good a grace as he could muster, and even went the length of joining with some heartiness in the time-honoured strains of "Reuben Ranzo." "After all," he reflected, "may as well do the thing properly while you're about it."

Still, he wasn't sorry when the time drew near for the little comedy to come to an end. Dropping, with a sigh of relief, the rope on which he had been hauling he walked quickly off towards the poop, rubbing his fat palms tenderly as he went. They had so long been strangers to anything resembling a job of work that they were already beginning to blister.

"Well, Skipper," he cried gaily, "time to square our li'l' account and say so long, I guess!"

The captain gave him rather a peculiar glance, and led the way in silence down into the cabin.

Seattle Sam hesitated a moment. Time was getting short. But a drink was a drink, after all, and it would have meant going back on the tradition of a lifetime to refuse one.

He had hardly entered the saloon before he became vaguely conscious of a certain lack of cordiality in the atmosphere. The pilot's dirty glass was still on the table, but there was no other sign of liquid refreshment. He could not keep a note of uneasiness out of his voice.

"Well, Skipper," he repeated, "so long, and a pleasant voyage!"

The captain's eyes met his in a cold stare of absolute repudiation. Seattle Sam's extended hand dropped slowly to his side, and the self-satisfied smirk faded from his face. The captain had taken up a position between him and the companion. Instinctively he turned towards the alleyway which led to the main deck. It was blocked by the substantial form of Mr. Michael Doyle.

Too late the ghastly truth began to dawn.

"Talking about squarin' accounts," said the skipper slowly, "I've got a little account to square. It's been waiting a long time too. Matter o' fifteen years or so. Take a good look at me! Ever seen me before? Just cast your mind back a bit to the time when you were 'Frisco Brown's runner, and shipped a big husky apprentice out o' the Golden Gate in a Yankee blood boat that the 'Bride of Abydos' is a day-nursery to!... I've got the scars of that trip about me yet, soul and body, Mister Seattle Sam, and you're goin' to pay for 'em, and compound interest too!"

As he spoke, three long wails from the tug's hooter rent the air, answered by round after round of cheering from the ship.

The skipper stood back, while Seattle Sam dashed up on to the poop with a low howl of rage and terror.

The tug's hawser trailed dripping through the water, and she was turning her nose for home with a mighty churning of her paddles. The crimp rushed to the rail, waving his arms frantically above his head, and a yell of derision greeted him from the crew lined along her bulwarks. They were all in it, then! He was alone, alone, with a man he had shanghaied, a crew he had tried to swindle, and a sea-chest full of waste paper wherewith to face the bitter days and nights off the Horn.

"Bos'n!" yelled the skipper. "Call all hands aft!"

"Lay aft all hands!" roared the bos'n, and soon a throng of interested faces looked up at the captain as he stood with his hands planted on the poop rail.

His words were few but to the point.

"Boys, you've heard I'm a hard man to sail under. Maybe I am. That's for you to find out. I won't have back chat. I won't stand for any sojering or shinaniking. If you're decent sailormen, and know your work, and do it, we'll get on all right. If you're not, me and my mates are here to knock ruddy hell out of you.

"One word more. This man here"—he indicated the trembling form of Seattle Sam—"came on board my ship yesterday to sell you. I'll give you his words. 'I'll fool 'em I'm goin' to sign on myself, and they'll come like lambs. Twenty dollars apiece and the men are yours. And I don't care if you give 'em ruddy hell!' Now I say to you, 'This man's yours! Take him, and I wish you joy of your shipmate!'"

And, grasping Seattle Sam by the collar of his coat and the scruff of his pants, he propelled him to the top of the poop ladder and gave him a skilful hoist which dropped him full in the midst of the expectant group below.

The tug's smoke was a grey feather on the skyline; Flattery a grey cloud on the port bow.

The song of the wind in his royals was sweet music in Captain Bascomb's ears. So was the rush and gurgle of the waves under the clipper's keel. So were all the little noises that a ship makes in a seaway.

But, oh, sweeter far than them all was a confused turmoil which ever and anon came vaguely to his hearing—a sound made up of thuds, of cries, of curses—which indicated beyond the shadow of a doubt that Mr. Samuel Grover, some time of 'Frisco, and late of Cormorant Street, Victoria, was undergoing the decidedly painful process of being ground exceeding small!

PADDY DOYLE'S BOOTS

A FORECASTLE YARN

YOU know that junk store on the Sandoval waterfront? A Chink keeps it—Charley Something or other, don't remember the rest of his name. If you don't know the place I mean, you know plenty more just like it. The sort of place where you can buy pretty well anything under the sun, everything second-hand, that is; any mortal thing in the seagoing line that you can think of, and then some. That's Charley's!

Well, once Larry Keogh (every one used to call him Mike, because his name wasn't Michael), and Sandy MacGillivray from Glasgow, and a Dutchman called Hank were in want of one or two things for a Cape Horn passage. Their ship was the old "Isle of Skye." Did you ever meet with any of them "Isle" barques? They were very fine ships. There was the "Isle of Skye," "Isle of Arran," "Isle of Man," and a whole lot more I just forget—all "Isles." You wouldn't find any of them now. Some were lost, some broken up, some went under the Russian or Chilian flag, and the firm that owned them (MacInnis, the name was) went out of business at the finish. And as for the old "Isle of Skye" herself, she piled up on Astoria a little more than a year ago—foreign-owned then, of course.

Round these three chaps I was speaking about went to Charley's joint. Larry and Hank got what they wanted soon enough. At least, they got what they had money for, which wasn't very much, Charley not being in the humour to treat Larry as handsome over some lumps of coral Larry wanted to trade for clothes.

This Sandy MacGillivray I mentioned, however, was a bit of a capitalist, and he was also of an economical disposition; and what with wanting to lay out his money the best way and not being able to bear the feel of parting with the cash when he'd found what he wanted to buy, he had his pals with the one thing and the other teetering about first on one foot and then on the other, and sick to death of him and his shilly-shallying.

At long last he got through; and then nothing would fit but Charley must give him something in for his bargain.

"No good, no good!" says the Chink, looking ugly the way only a Chink can. "You pay me, you go 'long!... P'laps I give you somet'ing you no like."

He grinned and showed his dirty yellow teeth.

"Ut's not possible," said Larry. "Sandy's the one that'll take it, if it's neither too hot nor too heavy."

"All light," says the Chink, sulky-like. "I give you velly good pair o' boots."

Hank's eyes nearly popped out of his head, and so did Larry's, when they saw what Sandy had got through just having the gall to ask.

A beautiful pair of sea-boots they were, and brand-new, or very near it, by the look of them. Sandy thought the old fellow was joshing him; but it was all right. He was nearly beside himself with delight. He stopped outside a saloon once on the way to the ship, and stood turning over his money in his pocket so long that the boys began to think he was going to celebrate his good fortune in a fitting manner.

But all he said at the finish was, "It's a peety to change a five spot. Once change your money an' it fair melts awa'"

Larry sighed. If he'd known about those boots he might have had a bid for them. And now Sandy had got them for nothing. Larry made him a sporting offer of his coral in exchange for them, but it was no go.

"To hell wid ye for a skin-louse!" says Larry, who was getting a bit nasty by this time. He had a great thirst on him, and no money to gratify it, and that was the way it took him. "Ye'd take the pennies off your own father's eyes, so you would, and he lying dead."

Sandy showed the boots to the rest of the crowd, and of course every one had something to say. But there could be no doubt he had got a wonderful fine bargain.

"I wouldn't wonder but they have a hole in them," said Larry. The notion seemed to brighten him up a whole lot. "The water will run in and out of them boots the way you'll wish you never saw them. I know no more uncomfortable thing than a pair of boots and they letting in water on you."

Sandy was a bit upset by this idea of Larry's, so he filled the boots with water to see if there was anything in it. Leak—not they!

"It would be a good thing," said Larry with a sigh, he was that disappointed, "if the old drogher herself was as seaworthy as them boots. As good as new they are, and devil a leak is there in ayther one of them. But maybe," he went on, cheering up again a bit, "maybe some person has been wearing them that died of the plague. It is not a very pleasant thing, now, to die of the plague. I would not care to be wearing a pair of boots and I not knowing who had them before me."

"Hee-hee," sniggers Sandy in a mean little way he had. "Hee, hee—ye'll no hae the chance o' wearin' these."

And then it was that old Balto the Finn—he was an old sailorman, this Balto, and he could remember the real ancient days, the Baltimore clippers and the East Indiamen—spoke for the first time.

"From the dead to the dead!" says Balto. "From a dead corpse were they taken, and to a dead corpse will they go."

They are great witches, are Finns, as every one knows. And it seemed likely enough that the first part of the saying, at least, was true, for old Charley hadn't the best of names for the way he got hold of his stuff.

Sandy was one of those chaps who go about in fear and trembling of being robbed; so, after he saw how all the crowd admired the boots, he took to wearing them all the time ashore and afloat. He went ashore in them the night before the "Isle of Skye" was to sail.

He came aboard in them, too, that same night....

The tide drifted him against the hawser, and the anchor watch saw him and hauled him in. Dead as nails, was poor Sandy, and no one knew just how it came about. It was thought he'd slipped on the wet wharf—it was a very bad wharf, with a lot of holes and rough places in it. And of course a man can't swim in heavy boots....

There was a man in the "Isle of Skye" at that time, a Dago. His name was Tony, short for Antonio. He bought Sandy's boots very cheap, no one else seeming to care for them.

That was a cruel cold passage, and the "Isle of Skye" being loaded right down to her marks, she was a very wet ship indeed. So that the time came when more than one in the starboard watch wished they were in that Dago's boots after all, and the fanciful feeling about poor Sandy began to wear off.

The Old Man was a holy terror for cracking on: he had served his time in one of the fast clippers in the Australian wool trade, and he never could get it out of his head that he had to race everything else in the nitrate fleet. He would sooner see a sail carry away any day than reef it, and this passage he was worse than ever.

However, it came on to blow so bad, just off the pitch of the Horn, that the mate went down and dug the hoary old scoundrel out of his sweet slumbers, he having dared anybody to take a stitch off her before turning in. He cursed and he swore; but the end of it was that the watch laid aloft to reef the fore upper-topsail, and it was then that this Dago Tony, who was swanking it in the boots as usual, put his foot on a rotten ratline, and down he came, boots and all.

There was a lot of talk, and no wonder, about the things which had happened since Sandy MacGillivray got those boots from the Chink; and the Old Man getting wind of it, he told Sails to stitch up Tony boots and all, so as to stop the talk for good.

"Mind ye," said the Old Man, "Ah dinna hold wi' Papish suppersteetions, but there's no denyin' the sea's a queer place."

Nobody ever expected to see or hear any more of Sandy Mac's boots. But there was a man in the starboard watch that nobody liked—a sort of soft-spoken, soft-handed chap we called Ikey Mo; because he was so fond of stowing away stuff in his chest every one thought he had a bit of the Jew in him.

The day we sighted the Fastnet this fellow showed up in a pair of sea-boots.

"Where had ye them boots, Ikey, and we rowling off the pitch of the Horn?" asked Larry when he saw them. "It's a queer thing ye never wore them sooner."

"If I'd wore 'em sooner," says Ikey, "like as not you'd have borrowed the lend of 'em, an' maybe got drowned in 'em," he says, "and then where should I have been?"

"I would not," says Larry. "I would not borrow the lend of the fill of a tooth from a dirty Sheeny like yourself. 'Tis my belief you took them boots off the poor dead corpse they belonged to; and by the same token, if they walk off with you to the same place he's gone to, it's no more than you deserve."

The tale soon got round that Ikey had stolen the boots off the dead Dago, and it made a lot of feeling against him. But he only laughed and sneered when folks looked askance at him, and at last he left off making any secret of the thing he'd done.

"Call yourselves men!" says he. "And scared of a little dead rat of an Eyetalian that was no great shakes of a man when he was livin'!"

"Let the fool have his way!" says old Balto the Finn. "From a dead corpse were they taken, to a dead corpse will they go."

Very, very foggy it was in the Mersey when we run the mudhook out. I don't think I ever saw it worse.

Ikey didn't care. He was singing at the top of his voice as the shore boat pushed off:

"We'll furl up the bunt with a fling, oh ...
To pay Paddy Doyle for his boo-oots...."

"Who said 'boots'?" he shouted, standing up in the boat with his hands to his mouth. "Where's the dead corpse now?"

The fog swallowed up the boat whole, but we could hear his voice coming through it a long while, all thick and muffled:

"We'll all drink brandy and gin, oh ...
And pay Paddy Doyle for his boots...."

The tug that cut the boat in two picked up five men of the six that were in her. And the one that was missing was a good swimmer, too.

But then ... a man can't swim ... in heavy boots..

THE UNLUCKY "ALTISIDORA"

I

WHEN first the legend of the Unlucky "Altisidora" began to take its place in the great unwritten book of the folk-lore of the sea, old shellbacks (nodding weather-beaten heads over mugs and glasses in a thousand sailortown taverns from Paradise Street to Argyle Cut) were wont to put forward a variety of theories accounting for her character, according to the particular taste, creed, or nationality of the theorizer for the time being.

Her keel was laid on a Friday.... Someone going to work on her had met a red-haired wumman, or a wumman as skenned (this if the speaker were a Northumbrian) and hadn't turned back.... Someone had chalked "To Hell with the Pope" (this if he were a Roman Catholic) or, conversely, "To Hell with King William" (in the case of a Belfast Orangeman) on one of her deck beams.... There was a stiff 'un hid away somewheres inside her, same as caused all the trouble with the "Great Eastern."... And so on, and so forth, usually finishing up with the finely illogical assertion that you couldn't expect nothink better, not with a jaw-crackin' name like that!

Anyhow, unlucky she was, you couldn't get away from it! Didn't she drownd her first skipper, when he was going on board one night in 'Frisco Bay? Didn't her second break his neck in Vallipo, along of tumbling down an open hatch in the dark? Come to that, didn't she kill a coupler chaps a week when she was buildin' over in Wilson's Yard, Rotherhithe? Didn't she smash up a lumper or two every blessed trip she made? Hadn't she got a way of slipping fellers overboard that sneaky and sly-like no one knowed they was gone until it come coffee time and they wasn't there?... Say the skipper was drunk—well, ain't skippers gone on board canned up afore now and *not* been drownded?... Say it was somebody's business to see that there hatch was covered or else a light left alongside of it—well, ain't hatches been left open in other ships without folks walkin' into 'em into the dark?... Say it was only two fellers as was killed workin' on her—well, ain't there been plenty o' ships built what *nobody* got killed workin' on? Answer me that!...

So the Unlucky "Altisidora" she became from London River to the Sandheads—a legend to endure in many an ancient memory long after her bones were rust.

It was in the South-West India Dock that Anderton first set eyes on her—the sun going down behind Limehouse Church tower in a great flaming splendour, and lighting up the warehouses, and the dock, and the huddle of shipping, with an almost unearthly glory.

Anderton was in great spirits. He had waited a long and weary while for a ship; haunting the docks and the shipping offices by day, and spending his evenings—for he had no friends in London and no money to spare for the usual shore diversions—in the dark little officers' messroom at the Sailors' Home in Well Street and the uninspiring society of a morose mate from Sunderland, who passed the time toasting lumps of cheese over the fire in order—so he confided to Anderton in a rare burst of eloquence—to get his money's worth out of the damn place. So that when there dropped suddenly, as it were out of the summer heavens, the chance of going as second mate in the "Altisidora" he fairly trod on air.

It happened in this wise. He had spent a desolating morning tramping round the docks, offering his valuable services to shipmasters who were sometimes indifferent, sometimes actively offensive, but without exception entirely unappreciative. He was beginning to feel as if the new second mate's ticket of which he had been so inordinately proud were a possession slightly less to his credit than a convict's ticket-of-leave. Two yards of bony Nova Scotian, topped by a sardonic grin, had asked him if he had remembered to bring his titty-bottle along; and a brawny female, with her hands on her hips, bursting forth upon him from a captain's cabin, inquired if he took the ship for an adjectived day nursery.

He had just beaten a hasty retreat after this last devastating encounter with what dignity he could muster, and was all but resolved to give up the fruitless quest and ship before the mast, when he heard a voice behind him shouting "Mister! Hi, mister!"

At first Anderton took no notice. For one thing, he was far too much taken up with his own concerns to be much interested in the outside world; for another, he was not long enough out of his apprenticeship to recognize at once the appellation of "Mister" as one likely to apply to himself. And in any case there seemed no reason at all why the hail should be intended for him. It was not, therefore, until it had been repeated several times, each time a shade more insistently, until, moreover, he realized that there was no one else in sight or earshot for whom it could conceivably be intended, that the fact forced itself upon his consciousness that he was the "Mister" concerned, and he stopped to let the caller come up with him. He did so puffing and blowing. He was a round, insignificant little man, whom Anderton remembered now having seen talking to the mate of one of the ships he had visited earlier in the day.

"I say," he gasped, as soon as he was within speaking distance, "aren't you—I mean to say, don't you want a second mate's berth?"

Did he want a second mate's berth, indeed? Did he want the moon out of the sky—or the first prize in the Calcutta Sweep—or the Cullinan diamond—or any other seemingly unattainable thing? He retained sufficient presence of mind, however, not to say so, and (he hoped) not to look it either, admitting, with a creditable attempt not to sound too keen on it, that he did in fact happen to be on the look out for such an opening.

"Ah, that's good," said the stranger, "because, as a matter of fact, I—it's most unfortunate, but my second mate's met with an accident, and the ship sails to-morrow. Could you join to-night?"

Manage it? Anderton repressed an impulse to execute a double shuffle on the edge of the dock, to fling his arms round the little man's neck and embrace him, to cast his cap upon the stones and leap upon it. Instead, he said, with the air of one conferring a favour, that he rather thought he might.

"All right, then ... ship 'Altisidora' ... South-West India Dock ... ask for Mr. Rumbold ... tell him you've seen me ... Captain Carter."

Anderton stood staring after his new captain for several minutes after his stubby figure had disappeared among the sheds. The thing was incredible. It was impossible. It must be a dream. Here, only two minutes before, he had been walking along seriously meditating the desirability of taking a plunge into the murky waters of the London Docks, and in the twinkling of an eye, as it were, the whole aspect of life had been changed by a total stranger offering him—more, positively thrusting upon him—the very thing he had trudged the docks in search of until his boot-soles were nearly through.

If he had had time to reflect upon this bewildering gift thrown at him by wayward fortune it might have occurred to him that—like so many of that freakish dame's bounties—there was a catch in it somewhere. He might have thought, for example, that it was, to say the least, a surprising fact that—at a time when he knew from bitter personal experience that the supply of highly qualified and otherwise eminently desirable second mates evidently greatly exceeded the demand—a distracted skipper should be rushing round the docks looking for one. But no such idea as yet damped the first fine flush of his triumph. Why, indeed, should it? The ship's name conveyed no sinister meaning to his mind. He had never heard of her reputation; if he had, he wouldn't have cared a button.

He was, as it happened, destined to get the first hint of it within a very few minutes. Just outside the dock gates he ran into Dick Charnock, who had been senior apprentice in the old "Araminta" when Anderton was a first voyager. Charnock was now mate—chief officer he called himself—of a stinking little tub of a steam tramp plying to the Mediterranean ports; and Anderton, remembering the airs he had been wont to give himself in bygone days, took a special pleasure in announcing his good fortune.

Charnock blew his cheeks out and said:

"O-oh—*her*!"

"Well?" said Anderton a trifle huffily. "What about her?"

No one likes to have cold water poured upon an exultant mood. "Beast!" he thought. "Jealous—that's what's the matter with him!"

"Oh, nothing—nothing!" Charnock replied hastily. "I was just thinking about something else, that's all!"

This was so obviously a lie that it only made matters worse, and they parted a trifle coolly; Anderton refusing an invitation to enjoy the pleasures of London that evening, as displayed at Wilson's Music Hall, at which he would fairly have jumped less than an hour ago.

The morose mate was still sitting in the messroom, surrounded by his customary aura of "frizzly dick," when he got back to Well Street and burst in upon him with his news.

He withdrew the fork from the fire, carefully inspected its burden and after an interval of profound thought remarked:

"O-oh—*her*!"

His "O-oh—*her*" was, if anything, more pregnant with meaning than Charnock's.

"Well?" snapped Anderton. He was by now getting thoroughly exasperated. "Well? What about 'Oh—her '? What's wrong with her anyway?"

The mate thoughtfully blew the ashes off his latest culinary triumph and thrust it into his mouth.

"She's no' got a gude name!" he said, indistinctly, but none the less darkly.

"Not a good name—what's that mean, pray?" demanded Anderton angrily.

"Just that," said the mate laconically, and went on toasting cheese.

Anderton flung out of the room in a rage. By this time his first enthusiasm over his unexpected good fortune had received a decided check, and it was with distinctly mixed feelings that he made his way Poplar-wards to make personal acquaintance with his new ship.

What was the meaning behind all these dark hints? Was this mysterious "Altisidora" a tough ship—a hell-ship? Her skipper didn't look like it, though, of course, one had heard of captains who had the Jekyll-and-Hyde touch about them—butter wouldn't melt in their mouths ashore, but they turned into raging devils as soon as they were out of soundings. Anyhow, he was ready enough for such contingencies. He had been reckoned the best boxer in the ship as an apprentice, and he would rather welcome than otherwise an opportunity of displaying his prowess with his fists.... Was she perhaps a hungry ship? He reflected with a grin that he had received ample training in the art of tightening his belt in the old "Araminta." ... Slow—well, a slow ship had her compensations in the way of a thumping pay-roll. He remembered the long faces the crew of his old ship had pulled when the dead horse was not out before she was on the Line.... Ah, well, he supposed he should know soon enough. One thing was certain, if she were the most unseaworthy tub in the world, he had no intention of turning back. His situation had been desperate enough to call for a desperate remedy.

There was some kind of a small disturbance—a street row of some sort—in progress just outside the dock gate, and, despite his impatience to see his new ship, Anderton stopped to see what was happening.

A queer little scarecrow of a man was standing in the roadway, shaking his clenched fists in denunciation towards the soaring spars of a lofty clipper, whose poles, rising above the roofs of the warehouses, seemed to stab the sunset sky.

"Oh, ye beauty! Oh, ye murdhering bitch!" he shouted. "Lovely ye look, don't ye? Who'd think to see ye that ye had it in ye to kill the bes' shipmate ever a man had?"

A passing policeman, thumbs in belt, casting a kindly Olympian eye on the little man, tapped him on the shoulder.

"All right—all right now—move on! Never mind about that now, Johnny! Can't do with you making your bother 'ere!"

The little man whirled round on him furiously.

"Johnny! Johnny is it? Isn't it Johnny I'm talkin' about, the bes' shipmate ever a man had—smashed like a rotten apple, and no cause at all for him to fall—oh, ye villain—oh, ye——"

Olympus grew slightly impatient.

"Come now, move on! Can't do with you creatin' no bother! Move on, I tell you, if you don't want me to appre'end you!"

The little man shuffled off, still muttering to himself, and pausing now and again in his zigzag progress along the road to flourish his fists at those contemptuous spars stabbing the sunset. The policeman, catching Anderton's eye, tapped his forehead significantly.

"Case o' Dhoolallie tap, as we used to say in Injer," he observed. "Round 'ere nearly every day, 'e is, carryin' on same as you saw. Chronic!"

Anderton asked him where the "Altisidora" was berthed. A look—was it of surprise?—flitted across his stolid countenance. Anderton could have sworn he was going to say "O-oh—her!" But he didn't. He only said, "Right straight a'ead—can't miss 'er——"

There were quite a number of ships in the dock, of which in those days a fair proportion were still sailing ships—ships from the Baltic with windmills sticking up amidships, Dagoes with brightly painted figureheads and Irish pennants everywhere, Frenchmen with their look of Gallic smartness and their standing rigging picked out in black and white; she was none of these anyway.

Anderton's eye dwelt longingly on the tall clipper whose spars he had already seen soaring above the sheds. There, now, was the very ship of his dreams! He thought life could hold no higher bliss for a sailorman than to stand upon her poop—to control her, to guide her, to see the whole of her lovely height and grace moving in obedience to his commands. He sighed a little at the thought, as he continued to scan the vista of moored shipping with eyes that hoped and yet feared to find what they sought.

"Right straight ahead." She couldn't be far off now—why, his ship must be lying at the very next berth to the beautiful clipper.

But there wasn't a next berth: the tall beauty was lying in the very corner of the dock. Already the straggle of letters among the gilt scrollwork on her bow had begun to suggest a wild hope he daren't let himself entertain. But now it wasn't a hope—it was a certainty! This *was* his ship—this dream, this queen, this perfect thing among ships! Why, her name was like a song—why hadn't it struck him before?—and she was like a song ... the loveliest thing, Anderton thought, he had ever seen ... rising up there so proud and stately above them all ... her bare slender skysail poles soaring up, up until the little rosy dapple in the evening sky seemed almost like a flight of tropical birds resting on her spars. She dwarfed everything else in the dock. Anderton had thought his last ship, the ship in which he had served his time, lofty enough; yet now she seemed almost stumpy by comparison.

He climbed the gangway and stepped on board. The steward, a hoarse Cockney with a drooping moustache under a pendulous red nose, and an expression of ludicrous melancholy which would have been worth a fortune to a music-hall artist, came out of his little kennel of a pantry to show him his room, and lingered a while, exuding onions and conversation.

"Nice room, sir, ain't it? Orl been done right froo.... 'Ard lines on the ovver young feller, weren't it? Coo! Cargo slings giv' way when he was right underneaf—a coupler 'underweight bung on top of 'im! Coo! Didn't it jus' make a mess of 'im? Not 'arf...."

So that was what had happened to his mysterious predecessor! Well, it was an ill wind that blew nobody good, Anderton reflected. Poor beggar ... still he couldn't help it ... and after all——

And it *was* a nice room—no denying that! Heaps of room for his things, he thought, remembering the little cramped half-deck of the "Araminta" which he had shared with five other apprentices three short months ago. The ship belonged to a period which had not yet learned the art of cutting down its accommodation to the very last possible inch. Her saloon was a grand affair, with a carved sideboard and panelling of bird's-eye maple, and a skylight with stained glass in it, and all the rest of her fittings were to match. It looked as if he were going to be in clover!

A series of tremendous crashes, accompanied by the falling of a heavy body, broke in upon the steward's remarks, and he started and looked round, his toothpick poised in mid-mouth.

"Coo!" he exclaimed. "'Ere comes our Mister Rumbold—and ain't he pickled, too?... Not 'arf!"

He vanished discreetly into his pantry as the originator of the disturbance came ricochetting along the alleyway, finally bringing up against the door-jamb of Anderton's room, where he came to a precarious stand.

He was a man on the shady side of middle age, with a nose which had once been aquiline and a sandy-white moustache yellowed with tobacco. The impression he gave—of a dissipated cockatoo—was heightened by the rumpled crest of stiff hair which protruded from beneath the shore-going straw hat which he wore halo-fashion, like a saint on the spree, pushed well back from his forehead.

"'Lo!" he observed with owl-like gravity. "You—comin' shee long'f us?"

Anderton said he believed he was.

The mate reflected a minute and then said succinctly:

"Gorrelpyou!"

Not being able on the spur of the moment to think of a really satisfactory answer to this rather surprising remark, Anderton took refuge in silence, and went on stowing his gear.

"I said 'Gorrelpyou!'" repeated Mr. Rumbold presently, with a decided touch of pugnacity in his tone.

Anderton supposed it was up to him to say something, so he said:

"Yes, I know. But why?"

"'Cos—thiship—thishipsh—unlucky—'Alshdora'!" replied the mate. "Thashwy. Unlucky—'Alshdora'! 'N if any man shaysh I'm drunk—then I shay—my lorshangemmen, I shmit if I can shay unlucky—unlucky— 'Alshdora'—I'm perfec'ly shober.... I'm perfec'ly shober—'n I'm goin' bed!"

At this point he let go of the door-jamb to which he had been holding, and proceeded with astonishing velocity on a diagonal course along the alleyway, concluding by sprawling all his length on the floor of the saloon.

"Wash marry thiship," he enunciated gravely, sitting up and rubbing his head. "Furnishershall over blushop. Tablesh—chairsh—sho on. Mush make inquirations into thish—morramomin'!"

Here he again collapsed on to the floor, from which he had been slowly raising himself as he spoke; then, apparently deciding to abandon the attempt to resume the perpendicular, he set off at a surprising pace on all fours, and Anderton's last glimpse of him was the soles of his boots as he vanished into his cabin.

He finished stowing his possessions, and then went ashore to make one or two small purchases. The sun was not quite gone, and the greater part of the dock was still flooded with rosy light. But the Unlucky "Altisidora" lay now all in shadow, except for the gilt vane at her main truck which flashed back the last rays of sunset. She looked aloof, alone, cut off from her fellows by some mysterious and unmerited doom—a ship under a dark star.

II

It wasn't long before she began to live up to her reputation. She started in quite a small way by fouling her anchor off Gravesend, and giving every one a peck of trouble clearing it. Incidentally, it was Mr. Mate's morning-after head that was responsible for the mess. But that didn't matter: it went down to the ship's account all the same. Her next exploit was to cut a hay barge in two in the estuary. It was foggy at the time, the barge's skipper was drunk, and the "crew"—a boy of sixteen or so—lost his head when the ship loomed suddenly up right on top of him, and put his helm up instead of down. But what of that? She was the Unlucky "Altisidora," or very likely the barge wouldn't have been there at all. Down went another black mark against her name.

The captain, in the meantime, had apparently gone into retreat like an Anglican parson. He had dived below as soon as he came on board, and there he remained, to all intents and purposes as remote and inaccessible as the Grand Lama of Tibet, until the ship was well to westward of the Lizard. This, Anderton learned, was his invariable custom when nearing or leaving land. Mr. Rumbold, the mate, defined his malady briefly and scornfully as "soundings-itis." "No nerve—that's what's the matter with him: as much use as the ship's figurehead and a damn sight less ornamental!"

Not that it seemed to make much difference whether he was there or not. He was a singularly colourless little man, whose very features were so curiously indeterminate that his face made no more impression on the mind than if it had been a sheet of blank paper. It seemed to be a positive agony to him to give an order. Even in ordinary conversation he was never quite sure which word to put first. He never finished a sentence or even a phrase straight ahead, but dropped it and made a fresh start, only to change his mind a second time and run back to pick up what he had discarded. And this same painful uncertainty was evident in all he did. His fingers were constantly busy—fiddling with his beard, smoothing his tie, twiddling the buttons of his coat. Even his eyes were irresolute—wandering hither and thither as if they couldn't decide to look at the same thing two minutes together. He had the look of a man on the verge of a nervous breakdown, and so, in point of fact, he was. He had jockeyed himself somehow into the command of the "Altisidora," through family influence or something of the kind, and had lived ever since in momentary dread of his unfitness for his position being discovered.

Anderton, for his part, owed to the skipper's invisibility one of the most unforgettable moments of his whole life. The pilot had just gone ashore. The mate was below. To all intent Anderton had the ship to himself.

A glorious moment—a magnificent moment! He was nineteen—not six months out of his time—and he was in sole charge of a ship—and such a ship. The veriest cockboat might well have gained a borrowed splendour in the circumstances; but here was no need for the rose-coloured spectacles of idealizing youth. Tier on tier, her canvas rose rounding and dimpling against the blue of the sky. She curtseyed, bowed, dipped, and rose on the long lift of the seas. Her hull quivered like a thing alive. Oh, she was beautiful! beautiful! Whatever life might yet hold for him of happiness or success, it could bring again no moment quite so splendid as this.

Mr. Rumbold, after a few days of the most appalling moroseness while the drink was working out of his system, developed, rather to Anderton's surprise, into a quite entertaining companion, possessed of the relics of a good education, a seemingly inexhaustible repertoire of unprintable stories, and a pretty if slightly bitter wit. He was perfectly conscious of the failing that had made a mess of his career. Anderton guessed from a hint he let drop one day that he had once had a command and had lost it, probably through over-indulgence in the good old English pastime known as "lifting the elbow." "A sailor's life would be all right if it was all like this," he broke out one day—it was one of those glorious exhilarating days in the Trades when the whole world seems full of rejoicing—"it's the damned seaports that play hell with a fellow, Anderton, you take my word for it! Drink, my boy, that's what does it—drink and little dirty sluts of women—that's what we risk our lives every day earning money for! It's all a big joke—a big bloody joke, my son—and the only thing to do is to laugh at it!" And off he went again on one of his Rabelaisian stories.

The ship fought her way to the southward against a succession of baffling airs and head winds where the Trades should have been, and a few degrees north of the Line ran into a belt of flat calm which bade fair to keep her there until the crack of doom. It wasn't a case of the usual unreliable, irritating Doldrum weather. It was a dead flat calm in which day after day came and went while the sails drooped lifeless against the masts, and men's nerves got more and more on edge, and Anderton began to have visions of the months and the years passing by, and the weed growing long and green on the "Altisidora's" hull like the whiskers of some marine deity, and himself returning, one day, old and white-haired and toothless, to a world which had forgotten his existence. To crown all, the melancholy steward at this time suffered a sad bereavement. His cat was missing—a ginger-and-white specimen, gaunt, dingy, and singularly unlovely after the manner of most ship's cats, but a great favourite with her proud owner, as well as with all the fo'c'sle. The steward wandered about like a disconsolate ghost, making sibilant noises of a persuasive nature in all sorts of unexpected places, which the mate appeared to find peculiarly irritating. The steward had only to murmur "P'sss—p'sss—p'sss!" under his breath, and out would come Mr. Rumbold's head from his cabin with an accompanying roar of "Damn you—shishing that infernal cat again! If I hear any more of it I'll wring your neck!"

But good and bad times and all times pass over—and there came at last a day when the "Altisidora's" idle sails once more filled to a heartening breeze, and the seas slipped bubbling under her keel, and she sped rejoicing on her way as if no dark star brooded over her.

The steward poked his head out of his pantry that morning as Anderton passed, with a smile that was like a convulsion of nature.

"Ol' Ginger's turned up again, sir!... What do you think of 'er?"

He indicated a small box in the corner in which a gently palpitating mass of kittenhood explained how Ginger had been spending her time. The prodigal in the meantime was parading proudly round the steward's legs, thrumming to the end of her thin tail with the cat's ever-recurring surprise and delight over the miracle of maternity.

"Artful, ain't she?" said the steward. "Right down in the lazareet, she was! Must 'ave poked 'erself down there w'en I was gettin' up some stores las' week. That's 'cos I drahned 'er last lot—see? Wot, drahn these 'ere! No blinkin' fear! W'y, they're *black* 'uns—ketch me drahnin' a black cat!"

Whether the advent of the black kittens had anything to do with it or not, it certainly seemed for a time as if the luck had turned. Day after day the ship reeled the knots off behind her at a steady fifteen. Every one's spirits rose. "Wot price the hunlucky 'Altisidora' now?" said Bill Green to the man next him on the yard. They were tarring down, their tar-pots slung round their necks as they worked. "There you go, you ruddy fool, askin' for trouble!" replied Mike, the ancient shellback, wise in the lore of the sea. "Didn't I tell ye now?" Bill's tar-pot had given an unexpected tilt and spread its contents impartially over Bill's person and the deck below. "If you was in the Downeaster 'Elias K. Slocum' wot I sailed in once, you'd git a dose o' belayin' pin soup for supper over that, my son, as'd learn you to play tricks with luck."

The luck didn't last long. Possibly a hatful of blind black kittens had not the efficacy as mascots of a full-grown black Tom. Ginger's progeny undeniably looked very small, helpless, squirming morsels to contend successfully against the Dark Gods.

The ship was by now getting into the high latitudes, and sail had to be gradually shortened until she was running down the Easting under lower topsails and foresail. Anderton had been keeping the middle watch, and had gone below, tired out, after a night of "All hands on deck." It seemed to him that his eyes were no sooner closed than once again the familiar summons beat upon the doors of his consciousness, and he stumbled on deck, still only half roused from sleep, to find a scene of the wildest confusion.

A sudden shift of wind had caught the ship aback. Both the foremast and mainmast were hanging over the side in a raffle of rigging, only the mizen, with the rags of the lower topsail still clinging to the yard, being left standing. The helmsman had been swept overboard, to be seen no more, and the ship lay wallowing helplessly in the trough of the sea, under the grey light of the dreary dawn—a sight to daunt the stoutest heart.

It was then that the mate, Mr. Rumbold, revealed a new and hitherto unsuspected side of his character. Anderton had first known him as a drunken and shameless sot; next, he had found in him an entertaining companion and a man of the world whose wide experience of life in its more sordid aspects compelled the unwilling admiration of youth. But now he recognized in him a fine and resourceful seaman and a determined and indomitable leader of men in the face of instant danger. The suddenness and completeness of the disaster which might well have induced the numbness of despair, only seemed to arouse in him a spirit in proportion to the needs of the moment. During the long hours while the ship fought for her life—during the whole of the next day, when the pumps were kept going incessantly to free her from the volume of water that had flooded her hold— when all hands laboured to rig jury-masts and bend sufficient sail to keep her going before the wind—he it was who continually urged, encouraged, cajoled, and drove another ounce of effort out of men who thought they had no more fight left in their bodies. He it was who worked hardest of all, and who, when things seemed at their worst and blackest, brought a grin to haggard, worn-out faces with a shanty stave of an irresistible humour and—be it added—a devastating unprintableness.

The ship managed to hobble into Cape Town under her jury rig, where Mr. Rumbold promptly vanished into his customary haunts, to reappear just before the ship sailed after her refit, the same sprawling and disreputable wreck he had been when Anderton first saw him. He never again showed that side of himself that had come to the surface on the night of disaster; but Anderton never quite forgot it, and because of the memory of it he spent many a patient hour in port tracking the mate to his favourite unsavoury resorts, and dragging him, maudlin, riotous, or quarrelsome, back again to the ship.

The "Altisidora" arrived in Sydney a hundred and forty days out. Her fame had gone before her, and she attracted quite an amount of attention in the capacity of a nautical curiosity. Moreover, the legend grew apace, as is the way of legends the world over, and has been since the beginning of time. Citizens taking the air on the water-front pointed her out to one another. "That's the hoodoo ship. Good looker, too, ain't she? Drowns half her crew every voyage. Wonder is anyone'll sign in her!"

And so it went on. She wandered from port to port, leaving bits of herself, like an absent-minded dowager, all over the seven seas. She lost spars—she lost sails—she lost hencoops, harness casks, Lord knows what! She scraped bits off wharves; she lost her sheer in open roadsteads and barged into other ships. She ran short of food and had to supplicate passing ships for help. When she couldn't think of anything else to do she even tried to run down her own tug. And yet in spite of it all—perhaps, for sailormen are queer beings, because of it all—her men liked her. They cursed her, they chid her, kindly, without rancour, as one might chide a charming but erring woman; but they stuck by her all the same. The old sailmaker, a West Country man who had lost all his teeth on hard tack, had been with her for years. "You don't mind sailing in an unlucky ship, then, Sails," said Anderton to him one day, when he was helping him to cut a new upper topsail to replace one of the ship's casual losses.

The old man pushed his spectacles up on to his bald head, and looked out over the sea with eyes flattened by age and faded to the remote blue of an early morning sky when mist is clearing.

"I rackon't ain't no use worryin' 'bout luck, sir," he said, "so long's there's a job o' work wants doin'."

From Sydney she went over to Newcastle to load coal for Chile, then on to 'Frisco with nitrates, 'Frisco to Caleta Buena again, over again to Newcastle, and last of all to Sydney once more to load wool for home.

III

Sixty miles west of St. Agnes Light the Unlucky "Altisidora" leaned to the gentle quartering breeze, homeward bound on the last lap of her three years' voyage.

Anderton stood on the poop, gazing out into the starry darkness that held England folded to its heart. Above him sail piled on sail rose up in the moonlight, like some tall, fantastic shrine wrought in ebony and silver to an unknown and mysterious god. The water slipped past her silently as a swimming seal, with a faint delicate hiss like the tearing of silk as the clipper's bow cleft it. His mind ran now forward, now backward, as men's minds do when they are nearing one of the milestones of life.

He remembered almost with a pang of regret the heady exultation which had been his when he stood on this poop alone for the first time, realizing that something had slipped away from him unnoticed which he could never hope to recapture this side the grave. Three years is a long while, especially to the young; but it was not in point of actual time, but in experience, that so wide and deep a gulf yawned between himself and the boy who three years since had left these shores he was now approaching. She had taught him many things, that old ship—more, perhaps, than he himself knew....

Rumbold wandered up on to the poop and began to tell smutty tales. The restlessness which always consumed him when the ship was nearing land was strong on him. Anderton felt a great pity for him. It would be the old tale, he supposed, as soon as the ship was made fast: this man, who had it in him to fight a losing game with death with a laugh on his lips, would become to the casual observer, a lewd, drunken blackguard, wallowing in the lowest gutters of Sailortown. What would become of him, he wondered—picturing him dropping steadily lower and lower on the ladder, driven to take a second mate's berth, thence dropping to bos'n, last to seaman—so on until some final pit of degradation should swallow him up for ever?

The man was in so queer a mood that Anderton hesitated about leaving the deck to him. But he reflected that he would have little chance of rest when she was fairly in the Channel, and decided to go down for a stretch off the land, so as to have his wits about him when they were most needed.

He did not know how long he had been asleep when he woke with a start. The ship's bells were just striking. He counted the strokes—three double, one single—seven bells. He might as well go on deck now. She must have made a landfall by now.

An inexplicable premonition had come over him, which he refused to admit even to himself, that all was not well. He listened: the ship still held on her course. There was no sound but the restless chirp of a block somewhere aloft, the creak of a yard moving against the parrals, the constant "hush-hush" of the waves as they hastened under the keel. He slipped into his coat and passed out into the saloon.

The lamp over the table was still burning smokily, mingling its light with the cold grey light of morning, and giving to the scene that air of desolation which perhaps nothing else can impart so completely. The place reeked of drink. Under the lamp, sprawling half across the table, was Rumbold. One whisky bottle lay on the floor, another on the table beside his hand, from which the last dregs spattered lazily to the floor.

The swine—the drunken swine! Anderton seized him by the arm and shook him furiously.

Rumbold lifted his ravaged face from the table and stared at him stupidly.

"Thish bockle'sh—water o' knowledge—good'n' evil," he said inanely. "Mush make—inquirations—morramornin'!"

His head dropped on his arms again.

Anderton took the companion in a couple of bounds.

It was like stepping out into wet cotton-wool. The stars were gone. The sky was gone, but for one pale high blue patch right overhead. The ship disappeared into the fog forward of the after hatch as completely as if she had been cut in two. There wasn't a soul to be seen but the man at the wheel, a stolid young Finn who would go on steering the course that had been given him until the skies fell.

Anderton started to run forward, shouting as he went; and his voice, tossed back at him out of the dimness, hit him in the face like a stone.

The next moment, the ship had struck.

She took the ground, so it seemed at the time, quite gently: with hardly a jar, hardly a tremor, only with a little delicate contented shiver all through her graceful being, like someone settling down well pleased to rest. You might almost fancy that she said to herself:

"There—I have done with it all at last—done with bearing the blame of your sins and follies, your weakness, your incapacity, your drunkenness, your indecision. I have been your scapegoat too long. Henceforward, bear your own burdens!"

And just then the mist rolled off like a curtain. She was right under the land, in the midst of a great jagged confusion of rocks that reached out to sea for nearly a quarter of a mile. The wonder was she had not struck sooner. You could see the pink tufts of thrift clinging to the cliff face, the streaks of green and yellow lichen on the rock, the thin line of soil crested with grass at the top. Above, sheep were grazing, and there came the faint querulous cry of young lambs. A scene to fill a sailor's heart with sentimental delight under any conditions but these!

There was nothing to be done. The Unlucky "Altisidora" had paid her last tribute to the Dark Gods. The ship lay jammed hard and fast on a sunken reef, and was making water rapidly.

They left the ship at sunset. The skipper took his seat in the boat without a word or a backward glance; the mate—sobered for once—hung his head like a beaten dog. The melancholy steward carried the faithful Ginger in a basket.

"Ain't been such a bad ol' gal, 'as she?" That was the gist of the crew's valedictions. They set off in single file up the narrow path that led to the top of the cliff—an oddly incongruous little procession in that rural setting.

Anderton came last of all. One by one his shipmates topped the crest and vanished. But still he lingered. He wanted just for a minute to be alone with this old ship that had come so strangely into his life and was now to go out of it as strangely.

From where he stood he looked down upon her, lying almost at his feet. He could see all her decks, the poop, the galley, the forecastle head— everything that had grown so familiar to him through years of ship incident and ship routine. How friendly it all looked, now that he was leaving it! He wondered how he could ever have thought her the agent of Dark Gods—this patient, lovely, and enduring thing that had done man's bidding so long— like him, the instrument of forces beyond her knowing or his. How good it had all been—how good! The dangers, the hardships, the toil, the rest, the rough and the smooth of it ... the voices of his shipmates, the courage and humour of them, their homely faces....

She was part of his life, part of himself, for ever! He would remember in years to come a hundred little things that now he did not even know he remembered, yet which lay safely folded away in the treasure-house of memory, till some chance word, some trick of sun or shade, some smell, some sound, should bring them to light ... and he would say, "Aye, that was in the old 'Altisidora,'" ... and perhaps be silent a little, and be a little happy and sad together, as men are when they think upon their youth....

Was that what the old ship had been trying to tell him all the time—the secret that had fled before him round the world, for ever near, yet for ever just out of reach, like the many-coloured arch of spray that hung gleaming before her bows? That the hard things of life were the things best worth having in the end?... A big green wave that flooded over you, that took the breath out of you, that went clean over your head—life was like that. Run away from it and it would sweep you off your feet, smash you up against things, drown you, very likely, at the finish.... You had got to hang on to something, no matter what—a job of work, an idea, anything so long as you could get a grip on it—hang on like grim death, and the wave would go over you and leave you safe and sound....

The sky was full of windy plumes of cloud. A long swell had begun to thunder in from the west, grinding and pounding her with leisurely irresistible strokes like blows from a giant hammer. The sea, the breaker of ships, was already at his work of destruction. Soon there would be a roaring as of a thousand chariots along all the headlands, and the whole coast would be one thunder and confusion of blown foam.

A call came to him from the cliff-top. It was time to be going—time for him to leave her! Presently he too topped the crest, and, when he next looked back, he could see the ship no longer. The Unlucky "Altisidora" had passed from his sight for ever.

9 789368 096917